Reviews

"In *Cats, Ghosts and Gremlets*, Tarra Light takes us on a remarkable journey into other-worldly dimensions most of us spend little time contemplating. Capturing the mood of mystical tales like *The Hobbit* or *Pan's Labyrinth*, Tarra brings all of the wonder, mystery, and captivating nature of stories from times long past into our modern-day world. A delightful read, with lessons woven deftly throughout the lines of this magical tale, *Cats, Ghosts and Gremlets* will take you on an intriguing journey you won't soon forget."

—Christopher Harding, author, *The Reindeer Boy: A Mystical Journey into the Dreamworld*

"Very enjoyable and revealing, deep and thought evoking. I feel the folks who read this will gain much insight on all planes. It was very light but really addresses issues that are important to be aware of. I can't wait to read Book Three!"

—Laura Hurst, retired art teacher

Other Books by Tarra Light

Angel of Auschwitz
A Spiritual Memoir of Forgiveness and Healing

"In the past year there has been so much written about the Holocaust and its few remaining survivors, the subject has recycled up into the public awareness once again... Other books have been written, but yours is unique and different from most in one particular aspect: your ability to draw out of the horror of it all the power of healing, forgiveness and reconciliation. That transcends all the rest and displays the healing that the world needs so badly right now..."

—Reverend Marian Breckenridge, co-founder,
Northwest School of Religious and Philosophical Studies

The Princess of Freedom
Book One of *Cats Can Save the World*

At this time in history when life on Earth is threatened, it is imperative to prepare the children and teach them values that will set humanity on course to a healthier future for everyone. *The Princess of Freedom* teaches young people the living skills of forgiveness and tolerance so we may overcome our differences and live in peace and brotherhood. It teaches children to serve as caretakers of Mother Earth and its inhabitants, and to appreciate the beauty of our planet and the wisdom of the animals as guides and teachers for humanity.

The Time Doctor Takes a Vacation

Begin your journey now to a fantastic future, free from the rules of the world we believe to be real. Invoke the Spirit of Imagination as you visit the Time Shop and meet Archibald Ben Dillon, a Master of Time. Using the powers of mind, he can create the future, heal the past, and transform the very essence and nature of time itself.

Articles

Searching for Myself in a Time of Change, "Northern Journeys," Bonners Ferry, ID, Spring-Summer 2017, and "Rogue Valley Community Press," Ashland, OR, Summer 2016.

Decree for Peace on Earth, "New Spirit Journal," Seattle, WA, December 2007.

Language of Light: Language of Awakening, "The Open Line," Spokane, WA, September 2005.

Meditate For Peace: World Instant, "Country Activist," Humboldt County, CA, December 1986.

Website: www.TarraLight.com

Amazon author page: amazon.com/author/tarralight

Cats, Ghosts and Gremlets

Tarra Light

Earth Light Enterprises

Front cover design by Robert Bissett and Tarra Light
Author photograph by Jasmin Lace

ISBN 978-1986216012
ISBN 1986216012

Cats Can Save
the World

A Trilogy

BOOK TWO

Cats, Ghosts and Gremlets

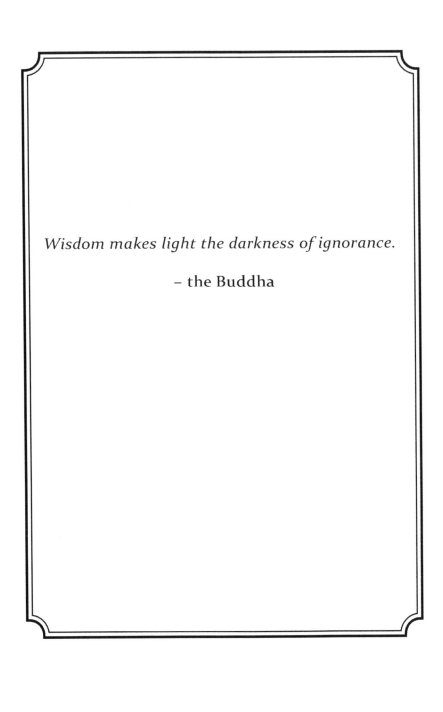

Wisdom makes light the darkness of ignorance.

– the Buddha

Our Responsibility

As you read the pages before you, open your mind and be willing to question everything. I am offering questions to ponder as you engage with the characters and themes of the story. You may ask yourself:

What do I value?
What is my responsibility?
How do I make conscious choices?

I wish to quote from American spiritual teacher Gangaji, who speaks so clearly of our responsibility for peace:

Human beings have been making war in every culture for a very long time. Culture is a reflection of the individual mind, and the individual mind is a reflection of the cultural mind. Since you are reading this, I assume you are interested in peace in your own mind. You are not waiting for *them* to make peace. This is good news, because wars are fought to get *others* to do it *our* way so *we* can live in peace. When you stop waiting for *them*, and instead shift your attention to your own mind, then you can recognize the tendency toward war in your own mind, the tendencies of totalitarianism, hate, revenge, and holding on. And you can recognize that those tendencies continue to deliver.

Somehow, in the face of it all, you find you want peace. You are sick and tired of the war within your own mind. You may even express it as a conscious prayer, a plea for help, for understanding, for deliverance, for grace.

Grace is here now. It is knocking at your door. You have a chance to be at peace in this moment. You only need to accept the invitation of your own heart, right now, regardless of inner or outer circumstances, and let yourself sink into the peace of your innermost being.

Unless all of us take responsibility for our own inner peace, the wars will continue. We cannot wait any longer for someone else to change. We cannot wait for someone to forgive us so we can forgive them. We cannot wait for someone to say they are sorry. Peace cannot be postponed.

—Gangaji, *The Diamond in Your Pocket: Discovering Your True Radiance*, Sounds True, 2005

Introduction

Originally written in 1993, on the cusp of the Electronic Age, *Cats Can Save the World* has transformed over time and morphed into a trilogy with *The Princess of Freedom* as Book One and *Cats, Ghosts and Gremlets* as Book Two.

The story recounts an episode in my life when I found myself thrust into a situation of homelessness, along with my husband, who was recovering from a back injury, and our three cats, Tiger, Princess, and Mirabel. Out of desperation, not knowing which way to turn, I accepted a position as caretaker of an old mansion, only to soon discover it was inhabited by mischievous spirits. They annoyed the cats and instigated arguments between the brothers that lived there.

Seeking to find a way out of our predicament, my husband and I engaged in impassioned dialogue, discussing and debating the existential questions of life. Can we create our reality? Is the future pre-determined? What is true? What is real? How do we know?

As Kriya in the story, I became a psychic detective, hot on the trail of truth. I launched an investigation into the causes of the boys' anger, which led to a deeper examination of the hidden forces shaping global events. As I taught myself to become a critical observer, more was revealed to me. I realized that the provocations of these unseen beings were an unrecognized cause of the wars that have plagued the human race for millennia. Observing the boys entranced by television programming, I recognized the power of the media to seduce the mind and motivate behavior from below the level of awareness. I feel it is my responsibility to warn people of the perilous course ahead if we do not claim our sovereignty, assert our free will and make choices from the heart. Let us not forfeit what is left of our democracy by making choices based on fear.

There is a way to a better world when we harness our spiritual power. I hope this story will broaden our perspective and open our minds to new possibilities. Humanity has untapped potential and it is time to rise to the challenge.

House of Mystery

Kriya strained to decipher the scribbled handwriting. "879 South Montrose Avenue," she read aloud. "We are here," she exclaimed expectantly. "We have arrived!" With cautious optimism, Tom rolled down the car window and peered ahead in anticipation. He and Kriya were embarking on a new life adventure with Destiny at the helm.

Positioned on the crest of a hill, the mansion overlooked the town of Meridian and offered a commanding view of the surrounding environs. Decorative designs embellished the walls, creating an impression of opulence and grandeur, declaring to all passersby that the inhabitants of this magnificent dwelling belonged to the cultured elite.

Stone gargoyles bearded with frost stood guard at the entrance gate, which opened to a stone pathway leading to the front door. Bordering the path on each side were ornamental gardens, once of exquisite beauty. Alas, the glorious flowers had shriveled and died in the autumn frost, skeletons of their former selves. It was the fifth day of November in 1993.

Together they walked down the path to face an uncertain future, Tom on crutches, Kriya by his side.

"Welcome!" Sunny smiled brightly as she opened the door. Her dreamy brown eyes revealed the mystique of an artist. A long black dress gathered at the waist accentuated her graceful feminine beauty.

Stepping into the foyer, Kriya suddenly recoiled, almost losing her balance. Then and there she had to recalibrate her energies to attune to the strange surroundings. Eerie vibrations emanated from the walls and the foundation, from the depths. A feeling of melancholy pervaded the ethers. Kriya felt ill at ease. She thought, *I sense a shadow presence. What is going on here?*

Tom froze up, catching the vibe, as Sunny chatted cheerfully on and on about this and that, oblivious to their distress. He thought, *Something feels out of kilter. Is this house haunted?*

"Come! I shall show you my artwork," volunteered Sunny, enthusiastic to the max. She led the couple down the hallway into the museum displaying her notorious creations. The walls were covered with her masterpieces—portraits of deceased family members who seemed to come alive after dark, as if the Spirit of the Night had breathed life into their souls.

"Follow me." Sunny led the couple to view a life-sized portrait of a distinguished gentleman with a serious demeanor. "This is my dear Uncle Daniel," she introduced him. "We were close, like soulmates. I was his confidant," she whispered. Her eyes welling up with tears, she remembered: "He disappeared mysteriously without a trace. I believe he was murdered. In fact, I'm sure of it, even without any so–called legitimate proof."

"What could be a plausible motive?" Tom put on his detective hat.

"Disclosure. That is my hypothesis. You see, Uncle Daniel was awarded high-security clearance by military intelligence. He possessed secret knowledge of mind control operations that the Controllers don't want people to know about. I suspect he blew the whistle on the deceitful Ministry of Information, which operates the propaganda mills that manufacture sugar-coated lies. Late at night, I sense his presence, waiting, lingering—for what I do not know."

A New Life

Shall I show you to your room?" Sunny smiled, pleased with the unfolding situation. Tom nodded. No comment. He was taking it all in.

Sunny felt Lady Luck was on her side that fateful evening when Kriya had visited her Women's Circle. They had appeared in each other's lives at just the right time. Kriya was in a predicament, her life turned upside down. Sunny was looking for a house sitter, and Kriya needed a place to stay.

As they approached the first flight of stairs, Kriya grabbed onto the banister, holding it tightly as each stair creaked under her step as she made her way upward and onward to a new life. She asked the Universe for guidance, *What am I to do? We were evicted from our dream home, Tom is still crippled from his accident, and the cats need a stable place to live. I don't see a lot of options for us right now. This is where our path is leading us, so we'd better make the best of it.*

They turned the corner on the landing and climbed yet another flight. Tom managed his way up the staircase leaning on crutches. He thought, *Everything happens for a reason, or so I've heard it said. Why did I lose my balance and fall off the ladder? Now I must watch my footing every step of the way.* A long hallway, three more steps, and they reached their destination—a small attic room at the far end of the house.

Thanking Sunny, Tom and Kriya dared to enter. The shades were drawn, and the air was stuffy, as if the room had been shut up for quite a while. Kriya ran to the window and wiggled it open to let in the fresh air. Then she sat on the floor and looked around, taking it all in. There was no furniture anywhere, not even a lamp for light.

"This is better than being homeless," Kriya supposed, trying to convince herself that everything was going to work out for the best.

"I hope the cats can cope with the spooky vibes," ventured Tom. "They are used to living in freedom, to coming and going as they please. Now they will be confined as indoor cats."

"Living here is going to be challenging for all of us," Kriya sighed.

Sunny

Sunny retreated to her sewing room, her sanctuary from the unpleasantries of facing reality. In the midst of the tools of her trade—sewing machine, ironing board, mannequins, and garment racks—she created a sacred space where she could dream and imagine. Walking over to the mirror, she smiled at her reflection, oh so pleased with herself and the life she had made.

Sunny lived the dream-life of an artist who creates a perfect world with their imagination, then sets up camp and lives in that world. A force field of denial held reality at bay. Anything that threatened her worldview was banished to the dungeon of her subconscious.

"Sunny" was her nickname. Her formal and legitimate name was Beatrice Marie Jameson. Everyone called her Sunny because she remained cheerful no matter what the circumstances. No one ever saw her cry. Ever faithful to her chosen reality, she thought, *Nothing goes wrong in my world because I can change it with my mind.*

She was happy to be who she thought she was. It was all okay with her. She sank into her rocking chair and drifted off into a fantasy world—images parading across the eye of her mind. Her attention wandered here and there until she became captivated by a framed photo of a Native woman on the side table. *Soon I shall be by your side,* she thought as she contemplated her imminent meeting with Dancing Eagle. The woman in the picture emanated a presence that drew Sunny in like a magnet. Soon she would be on the road, travelling to New Mexico to learn the medicine ways.

Introducing the Cats

Tom was grateful that Kriya was able to shoulder the responsibility of moving. She loved to plan and organize, and to set things aright. He admired her resourcefulness; she was unafraid to ask for help. She believed in the power of prayer to transform the circumstances of her life. She sought assistance from the downtown thrift shop, which donated the basic furnishings for their attic room: a bed, a table and two chairs.

~~~~

It was moving day! Kriya trudged up and down the long flights of stairs, hauling suitcases and housewares. At last it was time to bring in the most precious cargo of all—Princess, Tiger and Mirabel, who waited patiently in their carriers for the next moment to arrive. Kriya set out a bowl of water for her darling kitties. After carrying them to the room, she unlatched and opened the doors to all three carriers. With a loving eye, she watched her kitties inspect their surroundings, hoping their new home would meet their feline standards of approval.

Each cat was distinctive in character and temperament. Of Persian lineage, the lovely white Princess was bold and self-confident. Her virtue was courage. Trusting her inner guidance, allowing herself to be led, she dared to venture into unknown lands, far from the safe and familiar comforts of home. In a past life she was known as "the wizard's cat." Merlin the Magician was her mentor during times long ago. Her psychic powers had remained dormant within her. At the right time she would reclaim them and step into her power.

Mirabel was jet black like midnight in Zanzibar. Her virtue was patience. She knew how to wait. No trains to catch, no deadlines to meet, Mirabel had all the time in the world.

Tiger was a grey and black tabby with a bushy tail like a raccoon's. His virtue was presence. Tiger lived in the moment, taking pleasure in the here-and-now. He gave wise counsel to Kriya during her times of duress. Distraught over apparent failures, set back by disappointments, she sought his enlightened perspective on the events of her life. When her plans fell apart, he offered her guidance on the art of letting go. The "cat master" drew upon the wisdom of Heaven and Earth. He walked in balance because he had surrendered to the flow of the Tao. He radiated a transcendent joy that awakened the heart.

The cats had been transplanted into alien soil. What strange adventures awaited them in the house of mystery?

Sunny's Dream

Sunny was wild with anticipation as the day approached to leave for New Mexico. For years, she had envisioned herself in the Southwest living the life she desired. Her dream had come alive! She was about to fully inhabit the dream she had been living in her mind's eye.

Her skirt swished and swayed as she scurried about the house, up and down the stairs, washing, ironing, packing, and making the final preparations for her long-awaited journey. On the morning of her departure, Kriya helped Sunny carry her travel bags and belongings to the car and load them into the trunk. A three-gallon water jug. A Coleman cooler. A box of apples. Trail mix, freeze-dried meals, notebooks, camera, and so on. On top of the suitcases and supplies, she lay blankets, pillows, jackets, and a goose down sleeping bag.

"Good-bye, Kriya," Sunny yelled through the partly open car window as she turned the ignition key. "I know you will do a great job taking care of the house. Thank you so much! I'll call you from New Mexico."

The Warning

Kriya stood on the sidewalk watching Sunny drive away. Her car turned a corner and disappeared from sight. At long last Kriya felt a sense of relief. *I hope my life will be easier now,* she was thinking. *I hope things will sort themselves out.*

She closed the gate and walked down the path, contemplating her new surroundings. Bathed in the glow of the golden sun, Sunny's house appeared admirably beautiful to the undiscerning eye. Sunny had a clever sense of invoking the power of illusion. The outside of her house was designed to give passersby the impression of normalcy. But within these walls lurked a shadow presence that attempted to interfere in the lives of the people that lived there.

The relentless stress had zapped Kriya's strength. That night she went to bed early, desiring to rekindle her weary spirit. Her will was strong even though her body was frail. A mountain of obstacles could not dampen her determination to find a solution to their predicament. She believed in her own power to achieve her goals and create the life she wanted to live.

~~~~

Rap! Tap! Tap! Loud knocking on the attic door disrupted their dreamland journeys. Kriya jolted awake, sat up in bed and pulled the covers tight around her. Tom reached for his crutches and walked to the door, cautiously cracking it open. He saw two sets of eyes, two disheveled young men, taking a confrontational stance.

"Who are you?" Tom asked suspiciously. "It's the middle of the night, don't you know?"

"Who are you?" the tall boy echoed with a contemptuous sneer. "We live here. This is OUR house! I am Marshall. This is my brother Malachi." Marshall portrayed himself as "the man in charge." He claimed as his birthright the privileges of dominant male power.

Malachi was reluctant. He stood behind and to the side. (He was thirteen to Marshall's seventeen.) Malachi dwelled on his anger. Society was to blame for the cruel and unjust way life had treated him. He hid behind pounds of body fat as armor to shield him from the pains of life.

The younger boy spoke this rhyme:

> *We warn you here,*
> *Don't interfere!*
> *We declare and claim:*
> *This is our domain.*

"We are house sitters. I am Tom. I am here with my wife, Kriya," he answered. "Sunny didn't tell us anyone else was living here."

"A crime of omission, I see," Marshall replied. "Mom is like that. She forgets. And assumes. You have to connect the dots." With these words, the boys backed away and left the scene.

Closing the door securely behind him, Tom sat down on the bed next to Kriya, placing his arm around her, pulling her close. "That was a threat. We have been warned."

"Why didn't Sunny tell us? What are we supposed to do?"

"God only knows," Tom threw up his hands. "Let's sleep on it and see what the morning brings."

"How can you be so calm?" Kriya got out of bed and began pacing the floor. "I just can't turn off my feelings and go to sleep. I never would have agreed to house-sit if I had known we would be responsible for two teenage boys."

"Well, here we are. We need to see this through come hell or high water. It's only for three weeks."

"I should have asked Sunny more questions before blindly moving here and placing our lives in danger. If only I hadn't panicked when I read the eviction notice," Kriya was full of regret.

"We'd better not make decisions from a place of desperation; I see that now. Fear limits our vision of what we believe can be possible," Tom attested.

"Well, I tried to come up with alternatives before accepting Sunny's offer. This was the only opportunity I could see. Next time, I will think things through and not make assumptions."

"That makes a lot of sense."

Memories

Kriya resolved to stay calm in spite of temptations to the contrary. *I have made my way through all sorts of calamities,* she reminded herself. *I am a survivor.* A few days later, she was running errands in downtown Meridian. Shopping was a distraction for her, a welcome escape from the creepy vibes pervading the house. Before returning, she stopped for a cup of espresso at her favorite café. Sipping the brew and mulling over their circumstances, Kriya allowed her mind to wander and drift into fantasy. She imagined herself living in a perfect paradise, a heaven of the mind.

While Kriya was out and about, Tom lay in bed, contemplating. He reviewed in his mind the sequence of circumstances that brought him to this cosmic intersection of fate and the world. He examined his life from an unforeseen vantage point now that his accustomed way of life had abruptly ended.

Soulful memories of neighbors and friends, dear to his heart, flooded his inner eye, enveloping him in a cloud of sorrow. He was despondent over leaving their home of many years, where he had planted glorious gardens he tended with love, showcases of beauty and design. *I miss the natural rhythm of country living,* he lamented. *A chapter in my life is closed forever.* His heart longed for the impossible—what could never be again.

He remembered the meadowlands in May resplendent with wildflowers, and the Great Nether Woods shrouded in mystery and magical allure. He remembered watching Princess romping through verdant spring grasses, her fluffy tail held high like a banner in the breeze.

Tiger curled up on the pillow next to Tom, providing comfort and companionship as he rested and healed. Mirabel escaped the trials and tumult of the day by hiding in the closet, amongst the overcoats, shoes, and accumulating laundry. Princess sat on the windowsill, unperturbed. The past was not a problem for her. She lived in the Now.

Kriya Meets the Wind

The next morning Kriya arose bright and early, excited to meet the new day; she was regaining her strength and enthusiasm for life. From the corner of her eye, she spotted the red, white and blue mail truck driving down the street. Right away, she stepped out onto the porch and collected a stack of letters. *Slam!* The massive front door blew shut behind her. The old mansion shook upon its foundation, and the three cats in the attic shuddered in their hiding places. The irreverent Wind laughed at her fear. The woes and worries of human affairs amused the cold-hearted Wind. It mocked humanity's resistance to change and its claims of dominion over land and sea.

No chains in the world could imprison the ubiquitous Wind, nor stop it from going its own way. The Wind greeted Kriya:

Whissh Ho!
Whoa Ha!

I am the Wind,
Free to come,
Free to go.

I disappear and then reappear.
Now I'm here,
And then I'm there.

Kriya wondered:

> *How does the Wind know which way to go?*
> *In which direction is it to blow?*
> *North or South, East or West,*
> *How does the Wind know which way is best?*

The Wind rushed in the front door and raced through the house, up the stairs, and into every room. "I have come to shake things up," declared the Spirit of the Wind. "I shall blow apart your neat concepts of reality. I shall sweep through your nice orderly world and turn it upside down. I am the Force of Change." Gusts of wind charged through the house, rattling the windowpanes, slamming the doors, and shaking the cupboards, where china cups clinked and clattered on their neat and tidy shelves. The warrior Wind had not a care in the world as it wreaked havoc in its wake.

When the Wind was on the prowl, the cats crouched down in their hiding places. Tiger darted under the covers and curled up next to Tom. Mirabel dashed into the closet and hid behind the laundry basket. Only Princess remained at ease since she identified with the daring spirit of the bold and audacious Wind.

> *The Wind was invisible,*
> *But it could see and hear.*
> *The Wind knew what was going on.*
> *It was brave and free from fear.*

Three Cats in the Attic

Once ever so joyful, Tiger's heart was heavy with sorrow. *A shadow has fallen across my path. I am not the happy cat I once was*, he lamented. The eerie vibrations in the house were disturbing to his sensitive nature. Fine-tuning his psychic radar, he scanned the house room by room, on the alert for the presence of danger. "Beware!" he warned his feline companions. "I sense nasty spirits are lurking in hidden places. Watch for snares and booby traps. Vigilance is the key."

The Spirit of the Wind spooked Mirabel as it whizzed up and down the stairwell, slamming doors and shaking up her sense of reality. She hid away in the closet, hoping no one would find her there.

Princess sat on the windowsill, undisturbed. She had no fear of astral beings, nor of the audacious wind. The Seven Sisters of the Forest had taught her the ways of the spirit world, and she felt confident in her knowledge and power. (See Book One, *The Princess of Freedom*.) She advised:

> *Fellow felines, don't be fools.*
> *Spooks and goblins don't follow rules.*
> *Keep focused on God's love and light,*
> *Fear not the spirits that roam the night.*

The Twin Gremlets

Kriya sat down in the TV nook and began sorting the mail, laying it out on the coffee table and dividing it up into three distinct stacks: bills, letters, and magazines. The beatific smile of a young woman on the cover of a magazine captured her attention. Her angelic eyes expressed compassion of heart.

In the background was a vista of parched fields of grain scorched by the blazing African sun. In her arms, she held an emaciated brown-skinned infant—one of the countless starving children on our planet who barely live, passing each day on the threshold of death. Wanting to know her story, Kriya began to read: *Chemeka had been called to minister to the unfortunate sons and daughters of humanity, to bring comfort and healing to the helpless, lost, and forgotten ones.* The article was uplifting, yet Kriya's mood dropped into a dark depression. Her concentration was interrupted by a string of nasty curses silently registering in her mind as thoughts.

> *Gosh darn!*
> *A thousand damnations!*

With clairvoyant sight, Kriya saw two tiny gremlets, each one perched on the rubber tip of the rabbit ears antenna for the TV. The red gremlet was engrossed in a game of solitaire. The orange one was chewing gum and blowing giant bubbles that broke across his crooked nose. They were three to four inches in stature and appeared as tiny dwarfs with potbellies. They had round green eyes, pointed ears, and long tails with tufts at the end. She overheard their conversation:

It's too dull in this here place. Let's get things hopping!
Hey lady! Hey you! Ha! Ha! Ha!

"Who are you?" Kriya dared to ask.

We are the twin gremlets. I am Alderon, answered the red gremlet seated on the tip of the left antenna.
And I am Algenon, said the orange gremlet sitting on the right antenna tip.

"What are you doing here in this house?"

That's right! That's right! You got it, lady!
What are we doing here? We resent our assignment to this
    hole-in-the-wall outpost in Small Town, USA.
We want to play hardball. This is sissy work.
Television junkies are too tame for us.

Aghast at this unexpected conversation, Kriya hurriedly gathered up the mail and left the room at top speed.

Hidden Predators

K riya, you look pale!" exclaimed Tom. "What has happened?"

Kriya sat down in the chair by the window, centering herself. She took a couple of deep breaths and explained to Tom, "I saw a pair of ornery spirits lurking around the television set. They were cursing all that is true and right with the world."

"Now I see why our nerves are on edge. Why does Mirabel hide in the closet? Why does Tiger burrow under the covers? Because this place is haunted. That explains a lot! But we are here and this is our life now. We must learn to cope."

Kriya proposed, "Let's change our point of view and look at things in a different way. For example, the little creatures were actually rather cute, except they were not at all nice. In their society, I imagine they were raised by mothers who didn't teach good manners. They were very rude!"

As Kriya performed her chores cleaning house, she kept on the lookout for Marshall and Malachi, cautious not to offend. She feared a confrontation with the aggressive teens could turn violent. Bursts of machine gun fire from the TV nook caught her attention. The boys were on the couch drinking beer and watching their favorite blood-and-guts adventure story. "Watching TV is terrorific!" shouted Marshall, laughing exuberantly. Positioned on Marshall's left shoulder was Alderon, fixated on the violence. Algenon was seated on Malachi's right shoulder, provoking anger in the younger brother.

Each gremlet had a long suction tube extending from its stomach that functioned like a vacuum hose, sucking up the angst of anger and the ethers of adrenalin, the energies released by Marshall and Malachi while in the grips of sensationalized violence. As the seductive power of the media entranced young minds, the pernicious predators puffed up from their evening feast of raw emotion.

The Den of the Rebels

In a windowless room in the basement, Marshall and Malachi had fashioned their rebels' hideout. They inhabited an underground world of their own creation, a place where they could thumb their noses at the rules and ethos of so-called civilized society. Angry at the world, victimized by life, they resolved to strike back at the perpetrators of injustice. In their subterranean refuge, they felt free to unleash suppressed urges and engage in forbidden behavior—smoking hashish, drinking whisky, and watching pornographic videos.

A torn-up couch with three legs was propped up against the wall. Figurines of disdainful goddesses stood petulantly on the coffee table scorning the virtues of middle-class mediocrity. The cinderblock walls were plastered with life-sized posters of cinema queens and gangster heroes with derisive smiles. The stale odor of cigarette smoke mingled with the fragrance of patchouli and frankincense.

The throbbing beat of a heavy metal band resounded three stories up in the attic room of Tom and Kriya. She leaned out the window and looked down below to see a crowd of young ruffians gathered on the back porch next to the rebels' hideout. Neighborhood bullies and their cohorts had assembled in the wake of Sunny's absence. A conclave of malcontents vented their frustrations, dancing to the drumbeat of defiance.

The phone rang in the sewing room. "Hi, Sunny," Tom answered expectantly, as he had been waiting at the appointed time for her phone call. "How is New Mexico?" *Pause.* "Dancing Eagle must be an extraordinary woman." At that moment,

Marshall happened to walk by the sewing room and heard Tom's voice through the closed door. Pressing his ear against the door, he strained to overhear the conversation. He surmised Tom was reporting to Sunny about their social defiance and delinquent deeds. "Your sons are holding a party for the young thugs in the neighborhood," Tom recounted. *Pause.* "Yes, I'll do my best."

Marshall walked away thinking about what he just heard. The fire of his anger was stoked by Tom's apparent betrayal. He plotted revenge.

The Power of Choice

During his alone-time, Tom pondered on the eternal questions of existence. "Does life have meaning? Are we here for a reason?" During their after-dinner conversations, he shared his daily musings and philosophical inquiries with Kriya. She was sharp in her thinking, and that is one of things he liked best about his wife. "Do we have the power to shape our destiny?" he asked.

"I believe we can become masters of our destiny rather than victims of our fate," she asserted. "We create the future by the choices we make now, and the choices we have already made. We have the power to imagine our choices into existence, assisted by our prayers and clear intention."

"As creators, we need to come up with a plan to get out of here," Tom was resolute.

"Okay, and part of the plan is creating a new dream to be lived," she was optimistic. "We need to commit to something to renew our passion for life. A dream brings hope. We can turn the page and start fresh. We can look at life from the vantage point of renewal."

"Yes, hope lets the Light in," Tom was enthusiastic. "We need to ask ourselves, *What do we want? What do we really want?*"

Stone Gargoyles

The ferocious stone gargoyles standing guard on both sides of the front gate protected the entrance from the intrusion of evil spirits. On the left-hand side, a serpentine lizard took its station on a granite pedestal, hissing at anyone who disturbed his equanimity. Poised to strike, a golden lion stood guarding the right side, baring his fangs and growling at suspicious passersby. When aroused, the gargoyles discharged a venomous vapor that repelled trespassers, who ran for their lives.

As clever as chameleons, the twin gremlets fooled the gargoyle sentinels. They tricked them into believing that gargoyles and gremlets belonged to the same family of creatures. They alleged that gargoyles and gremlets were related—as second cousins to be exact. This deceit ensured Alderon and Algenon safe and unimpeded passage into and out of the house.

The gremlets assumed strategic positions atop the menacing stone monsters. Alderon stood lookout on the pointed ears of the lizard. Armed with a slingshot and a pouch of barbed pellets, he was eager to attack anyone who crossed the threshold of his domain. Algenon lay curled up amidst the tangled locks of the lion's mane, snoring away.

Returning home late at night, Tom leaned on one crutch as he fiddled to unlatch the front gate. Ever ready to stir up mischief, Alderon stood up on the lizard's back, removed a barbed pellet from his pouch, pulled back the rawhide strap and aimed his shot at Malachi's bedroom window. *Ping!* He released it. As it rattled the upstairs windowpane, Malachi sprang out of bed and ran to alert Marshall. The boys dashed down the hall and crouched down behind the potted foliage on the third-floor landing, waiting to ambush Tom.

Riders on the Wind

Alderon tossed a pellet in his twin's direction, pricking Algenon on the head. Waking up from a deep slumber, the gremlet was stunned and disoriented. *Get moving!* shouted Alderon. *Let's make some mischief here and now!* Jumping down from their seats atop the heads of the stone guardians, the gremlets ran up the walkway to the front door of the house. Impatiently they waited at the threshold, pacing back and forth, waving their thumbs like hitchhikers looking for a lift.

As Tom opened the massive door, the boisterous Wind blew in with a rush and a gush, laughing all the way. The gremlets hitched a ride on the back of the Wind and gleefully rode the rambunctious current up the stairwell. They got off at the third-floor landing across from Malachi's bedroom.

Leaning on his crutches, Tom climbed two flights of stairs and paused to rest at the landing. The boys darted out from their hiding places behind the bushy potted plants that decorated the landing area. Alderon sat on Marshall's left shoulder. Algenon sat on Malachi's right shoulder. They goaded the youngsters to assail Tom, trying to induce a fear reaction. Marshall jumped in front of him, blocking his way. Fixating his eyes on Tom in a threatening stare, he rolled up his shirtsleeves and flexed his biceps in a display of male power. He proclaimed:

We hereby claim: This is our domain.
We told you once. Beware! Refrain!
Our timely warning you did not heed.
Now Sunny knows of our delinquent deeds.

Tom greeted each boy with a deliberate nod and continued on his way. Years of meditation practice had taught him to remain calm and cool. *I need to stay in my center,* he thought, *and not take it personally. I don't want to justify their anger by giving them reason to attack.*

Angry Vibes

A surge of anger cascaded down the hall and flooded the attic room. Tom could sense the boys' animosity. They didn't care what Sunny wanted. She was gone and they sought to rule the roost.

Tom shut the door behind him and leaned his back against it, letting out a sigh of relief. Kriya sat up in bed, alarmed. Searchingly she looked into his eyes. "Tom, you look stunned. What happened?"

"Marshall and Malachi ambushed me down the hall. They tried to provoke me, but I would not engage and play their game. I didn't give them the reaction they were looking for."

"They're angry at you for tattling on them," she surmised. "You fanned the flames of their anger by telling Sunny about their rowdy party yesterday."

"They were already angry before I came along. Being angry is part of their lifestyle and I'm just a convenient target," he supposed.

"Tom, you know that I'm afraid of the boys. Their anger scares me because I grew up with it. My dad was a rageaholic. He exploded in fits of rage at the slightest provocation. I don't know how my mom was able to survive living with him all those years."

"It seems the Hand of Destiny led you here to learn about anger and overcome your fear of it. I think the Universe does have reasons. There is an underlying intelligence that orchestrates our lives."

"I want to understand the boys," she replied in earnest. "If I can feel compassion for them, I hope to feel compassion for my dad and forgive him. I am determined to uncover the causes of their anger and discover how all of us can live in peace in this house. I am launching an investigation. Detective Kriya is on the job, looking for clues, searching for answers."

"So far, what are your results?"

"No conclusions yet. I'm just beginning. I think they are angry at society for holding them back. They want freedom of self-expression; they want to experiment with life. Instead, they butt their heads up against the rules and limits of accepted social norms. They have assumed a stance of rebellion because their natural inclinations are being thwarted."

"A good theory, my dear Kriya," he concurred.

"Here's another piece to the puzzle," she suggested. "Maybe they're addicted to the adrenalin high so they create situations that enable them to vent and release their anger."

Tom frowned, "These boys are headed down a dark path. I hope Sunny teaches them about the Light."

Spiritual Warfare

Continuing her investigation, Kriya had an inspired idea: *Perhaps by glimpsing into the psyche of their mother, I can gain insight into the angry behavior of her sons. By studying the emotions expressed in her paintings, I can open a window into her character and point of view towards life.*

Entering the art museum, Kriya felt an unsavory sense of depression. A feeling of melancholy permeated the room. She walked from painting to painting, tuning in to the persona in each portrait, the expressions on their faces, the moods and feelings conveyed. *Interesting how Sunny appears light and cheerful, yet her paintings feel dark and morbid*, she mused. *These people are suffering from a mysterious affliction.*

Kriya was drawn across the room, like a magnet was pulling her in a certain direction. She found herself standing in front of the life-sized portrait of Uncle Daniel, the man who disappeared without a trace. She looked into his eyes and sensed a presence, an aliveness, as if a spirit within the painting was observing her. *If only Uncle Daniel could speak to me now,* she fantasized. *I wonder what is on his mind. Does he have a message for the world?* To her amazement, his image divided in two and the foremost persona stepped out from the canvas and into the room. She gasped in surprise as he asked her, "Do you *really* want to know?"

"Yes, I want to know. What are you thinking? I am not afraid to hear the truth."

"There is a plan at work behind the scenes that few people know about," he began. "For millennia, the Forces of

Light and the Forces of Darkness have been engaged in spiritual warfare for control of Planet Earth. Because their operations are covert, they occur under our psychic radar. When people are blind to their existence, they may become pawns in the struggle rather than free actors on the stage of life.

"I think people look the other way," said Kriya. "They don't want to see. They have invested years in creating their world-view of what is and what can be possible. They don't want to let it go."

"The Light wants people to be free," Daniel was emphatic. "The Light is the guardian of the fundamental right of free will, protecting it from encroachment by the Dark. The Dark harnesses the shadow side of human nature to advance its assault on humanity.

"The Controllers are sowing the seeds of chaos and destruction. They work in cooperation with the media syndicates that implement their fear agenda. Time and time again, history has shown us that people are willing to sacrifice their personal sovereignty for promises of safety and stability."

"I hope humanity wakes up and sees how people are being fooled," said Kriya.

"It is time to face the truth. The survival of the human race depends on what people believe is possible," he suggested. "You see, young lady,..."

"My name is 'Kriya,' if you please. Spelled K, R, I, Y, A. Kriya!"

"My dear Kriya," he addressed her, "Will you serve as my messenger to get the word out? I want to disclose the secret agenda to oppress humanity. Perhaps you can write a book about it after you find a new home."

Daniel's ghost-spirit was asking Kriya for a favor. In fact, she liked the idea. "This might be right up my alley," she winked. "I love playing detective and searching for the hidden meaning behind appearances. Nothing is the way it seems to be," she philosophized.

"People need to take back their power," he asserted. "They don't see how they are being victimized through exploitation of their emotions." He explained, "The mainstream media manipulates the psyche to evoke intense emotional states. The discharge of emotions is the diet of predatory beings that prey on negative feelings. The spirit junkies of the unseen world get their fix from the hormones released from the pathos of human suffering.

"You see, Marshall and Malachi believe they are acting according to their free will choices. But their right of self-determination is being thwarted. They are provoked from below the level of awareness; they are being triggered subliminally, to express anger through violence. The children of today are becoming slaves to the seductive trance of technology."

"What is going to happen next?" Kriya wondered. "Do people value their freedom? Will they wake up, rise up, and see? Or will they take the bait and indulge in self-gratification?"

"The future is up to us. The choices of today are the seeds of tomorrow." With these words, he turned around and stepped back in, melding into the portrait.

Uncle Daniel

Kriya needed to get away for a while, to gather her wits and make sense of what just happened. She took a walk down Montrose Avenue and around the block, contemplating her surprise encounter. *Uncle Daniel was not really dead, was he? Was he a ghost? Was it his soul speaking?*

Kriya was excited to tell Tom about her adventure in the art museum. Entering the room, she sat down, closed her eyes and centered herself before saying a word. She saw what she saw and heard what she heard. "Tom," she began. "I am amazed. I spoke with a spirit man who lives inside a painting."

"Who did you just talk to? A spirit man in the art museum?" Tom's interest was piqued.

"It was Uncle Daniel. Maybe his body is dead, but his soul is alive. Do you believe me?"

"I don't doubt you, Kriya," he reassured her. "I trust your ability to discern the truth."

Tom recalled, "I remember gazing into the eyes of an Indian saint as I held his photo in my hands. I sensed his presence radiating light that penetrated to my core. It was an insightful moment that opened my eyes to see that consciousness transcends time and space."

"The physical world is only a fraction of what is real," she stated as a matter of fact, adding "My Mom had clairvoyant sight. She could see angels and talked to Ascended Masters. I inherited my gift from her."

Tom remembered Sunny's account of Uncle Daniel's demise. "He was murdered for what he knew. He was a whistle blower who gave his life for truth. What did he say?"

"He said the mainstream media is the mouthpiece of the Controllers who serve the Forces of Darkness. They manipulate us by playing on our emotions. We think we are free but we are not," she reported.

"He asked me to be his messenger. He wants to alert the people of Earth to unseen perils. He wants to reveal the secret agenda to help people see how they are being controlled. He stands for human rights and freedom for everyone.

"Living in this house, watching Marshall and Malachi, showed me the power of media to mold young minds. I shall dare to write the book that Daniel is suggesting. I shall expose attempts to undermine personal freedom and sovereignty. We shall lift the veils of ignorance and set the people free!" Kriya the Crusader was on the job again.

"Lucky he found you. This is more than coincidence. This is *meant to be*," Tom declared, as if this propitious meeting was a confirmation of his belief in destiny. He looked at his wife and saw a physically frail but determined young woman. Assuming a male protective stance, concerned for Kriya's welfare due to her sensitive and vulnerable nature, he warned her, "This is risky business. Will people believe you? They could pelt you with rotten eggs or even worse, and ruin your reputation as a sane person," he joked.

"I stand my ground as a messenger of Light," she proclaimed. "The secrets of the Shadow world shall see the light of day! I shall get the word out and tell the people what they need to know to be free. Then they can make wise decisions because they know the truth. Then they can take responsibility as aware beings."

"We don't want to become unsuspecting victims like Marshall and Malachi," Tom agreed.

Grizwald

A mong the spirit beings that dwelled in the old house was an astral predator assigned to Marshall and Malachi.

Grizwald was of Reptilian descent, and proud of it. Although he wasn't overly handsome as far as reptiles go, that didn't stop him from admiring himself and indulging in narcissism. With a distinctive look no other could rival, he flaunted his long snout and curved ivory tusks, displaying his bravado.

"The Griz" played secret games unbeknownst to Marshall and Malachi, as he manipulated their psyches for his amusement. In the world where he came from, the logical mind was the authority of truth. It was a world without heart where love was unknown.

The astute reptile zeroed in on the self-absorbed nature of the younger brother, and induced a sullen and morose quality to his temperament. He formulated thought-forms of victimhood and breathed them out through his long protruding snout, dispersing them in the boy's bedroom as a thick haze of despair. As sensitive young Malachi absorbed the negativity, he was overcome by a sense of powerlessness, accompanied by self-hatred and self-doubt. To compensate for his insecurity, he assumed the mantle of superiority and the stance of aggression, basing his power on mental prowess, muscle and might, rather than strength of heart and will.

Grizwald became bored with no one to taunt when the boys were at school or playing in the neighborhood. To pass the time, he reminisced about his home-world light years away. On

---

his planet, the reptile was King of the Land, as on Earth the lion is King of the Jungle.

The Reptiles were a warrior race adept at creating conflict. They travelled the galaxy instigating quarrels and provoking wars so they could reap the benefits. As legend has it, long ago, before the advent of humanity, a Reptilian force assumed control of Planet Earth and claimed it as their own.

Defeated

As dark clouds laden with undelivered rain raced across the winter sky, Malachi trudged home from school seething with anger. He had been turned down for a part in the school play, a role he dearly wanted and felt he deserved. His tender ego was crushed under the weight of society's rejection.

Once again, he did not make the grade. Once again, he was not good enough. The aspiring young actor felt victimized by the judgments of his peers and superiors. In the eyes of the world, he was a loser at the game of life. In his heart, he desperately wanted to be part of something bigger, even grandiose, but society was blind and could not recognize his greatness nor see the truth of him.

To be a great actor was his secret ambition. He wanted to be a star and shine on stage for all to see. But time and time again the Hand of Fate sabotaged his future. Acting was an avenue to escape his black moods and morbid imagination, and the torment of his soul. To transform into the character of the play, he had to let go of his self-image and sense of identity. It was freeing for Malachi to become somebody else for a few glorious moments on the stage of life.

Pierced by the sting of rejection, he created a wall of protection over his heart, shielding him from feeling empathy for the suffering of others. He retreated to his room, shut the door, and replayed his victim story in his mind, brooding over the injustice of society. Life had just given him one more reason to ferment his anti-social attitudes and distrust of the world.

The Griz hovered in the background, keeping a watchful eye on the young dissidents. Because he could read the thoughts and energy fields of each brother, Grizwald knew how to activate their trigger points to provoke animosity between them. Although the boys were unaware of his presence, Grizzy's unrelenting prodding produced a state of perpetual annoyance and irritability in the young men.

Malachi's defeat offered the perfect opportunity for The Griz to target him and create a tasty meal for himself of anger and despair. He sauntered down the hall to Marshall's bedroom and passed through the wall into the teen's domain. Marshall was engaged in playing solitaire, a game he liked to win. The cunning reptile projected an energetic cord into the auditory center of his brain, creating a telepathic conduit for Grizzy's malevolent thoughts.

Seemingly out of the blue, Marshall felt a sense of urgency to demean his younger sibling. He knocked on Malachi's door, unaware that The Griz was following close behind him. As the predatory reptile channeled a tirade of criticism, the older brother assumed he was listening to his own thoughts. Marshall berated Malachi, "You can't do anything right! You'll never amount to anything."

Malachi retorted, "I'm tired of your ridicule and mockery." A fight ensued between the brothers, as Grizwald applauded. Alderon and Algenon took sides, each rooting for their favorite teen.

Astral spiders dropped down on threads from the ceiling to get a closer view of the scuffle. Nefarious denizens of the underworld delight in the suffering of others. They sustain themselves on a diet of human misery.

Escape from the Gremlets

The gremlets had a field day while Tom and Kriya were in town running errands. In the spirit of mischievous fun, they taunted and teased their feline neighbors, whispering snide remarks into their innocent furry ears— poking fun at the kinks in Princess's whiskers, Mirabel's pointed ears, and Tiger's bushy tail and zigzag stripes. They sang their song:

> *We are the demons of the darkness.*
> *We linger in the night.*
> *We feed off anger, hate, and fright.*
> *We are the adversaries of the Light.*

Mirabel hid in the closet, crouching behind the laundry basket, leaving only to eat her kibbles and use the litter. Princess remained cool, calm, and collected, unruffled by the jeers and jibes of the troublemaker twins.

Tiger was the most psychic of the three felines. He was attuned to vibrations and could see and hear the spirit world. Ears laid back against his head, he listened as the rasping astral voices spewed out humiliating insults targeting Princess and Mirabel.

"I have lost my zest for life," Tiger lamented as depression set in. He wanted to protect Mirabel, who he saw as guileless and vulnerable. He saw how she suffered from the onslaught of negativity. "Let's get out of here!" he beamed to her telepathically. She heard his message in her mind and sent back her reply, "I'm with you. Let's go!"

Tiger reached under the door with his paw and carefully pulled it towards him. As the door slowly opened, he cautiously peered down the dimly lit hallway on the lookout for spirit predators lurking in ambush. He especially wanted to avoid a confrontation with the unholy gremlet twins.

Mirabel stood behind Tiger as he scrutinized the long passageway to freedom. "All clear!" he shouted in feline telepathy. The two adventurers darted down the hallway, rounded the corner and ran into the bathroom at the head of the stairs. Tiger searched for a safe place to hide and located a loose ceramic tile under the claw-foot bathtub. As he pried it out with his paw, he beamed to Mirabel, "We can hide in the wall. No one will find us here."

The bold escapees squirmed their way through the hole and found themselves in the dark dusty interior space between the walls. Long copper pipes were mounted on the framing studs. Electrical wires ran back and forth like highways of liquid light. The cats climbed up a four-by-four post and passed through an opening in the insulation, entering a large cavernous area housing the rafters supporting the roof. Here they made camp and settled in for the night.

The Power of the Light

In their hideaway amongst the rafters, free from the taunts and jeers of the annoying gremlet twins, Tiger regained his composure and his spark of life was rekindled. He tapped back into his power as the Tiger master who had offered wise counsel to Tom and Kriya, and the cats.

He sat high upon a sturdy beam under the peak of the roof. Mirabel sat below. She asked her Tiger teacher, "How can we benefit from encountering dark forces?"

Tiger closed his eyes and entered the silence of the heart. He answered, "As the force of opposition, they challenge us to overcome obstacles. They test our ability to discern the truth. They test our resolve to keep our hearts open. By passing their tests, we become stronger. Our enemies become our teachers when we heed the lessons they offer in the school of life."

"Are the gremlets part of God?" Mirabel wondered. "They are nasty and mean. I don't think God would approve of their rude behavior."

"God is all inclusive. God is Love, and Love does not judge."

"Which is stronger, the Light or the Dark?" inquired Mirabel.

"The light of a single candle can dispel the darkness of ten thousand nights," Tiger remembered an old proverb. "The Forces of the Light are stronger because Love is the greatest power in the Universe."

The Wind Doesn't Worry

*S*lam! went the door behind them as Tom and Kriya entered their attic room. The Wind followed them inside on a mission to make a "house call."

Princess was asleep on her velvet cushion when the Wind approached her. Gently blowing on the sleeping Princess, it aroused her from her slumbers. She greeted the Wind in salutation, then stretched into a few yoga asanas. Gracious as ever, she offered her velvet cushion for the Wind to take a nap and rest from its wanderings.

Tom laid his crutches against the wall and rested on the chair by the window. Kriya sat on the bed and began to fold the laundry. She noticed the room had an eerie empty feeling like something was amiss. Kriya looked around. Where was Mirabel? Where was Tiger? She looked beside Tom's pillow and Tiger was not there. She turned on the light in the closet and Mirabel was gone.

Princess sent her a mental message: "Tiger and Mirabel ran away from the nasty gremlets. No need to worry. You can place your trust in Tiger. He loves Mirabel and will safeguard her, like a chivalrous knight of olden times."

"And you decided to stay?"

"Alderon and Algenon don't bother me. I just ignore them. I see them, but I pretend that I don't. Then they leave me alone. So you see, there's no need for me to run and hide. They have no power over me," she explained. "I am happy being in the here-and-now, sitting on my window seat watching the grand adventure of life. I am free like the Wind is free."

The Wind is on its way.
It's going here.
It's going there.
The Wind doesn't care.

Hurry, scurry. Hurry, scurry.
The Wind doesn't worry.

"When I am real quiet inside and sit very still, no one knows that I am here," she whispered.

Cedar and Sage

During her sojourns in the Great Nether Woods near Tom and Kriya's house, Princess met a wise woman, a Sister of the Seventh Ray, who taught her the ancient art of smudging. The Sister had instructed Princess, "The energy around us affects how we feel and think. It is important to keep the energy clear in the space where we live."

Remembering her guidance, Princess telepathed to Kriya this mental message: "Let us perform a ritual of purification to cleanse this house of negative energy. Wash away dirt and grime. Let in the light, and the gremlets will flee to the hills. Then Mirabel and Tiger will sense the shift in energy and decide to come back."

"Great strategy, Princess." Kriya was impressed by her white cat's breadth of knowledge. She found the scrub brush and the wash bucket, the broom and the mop. Kriya sang as she worked:

> *Sweep and dust,*
> *Wash and clean,*
> *Sing a happy tune.*
> *Sprinkle rose petals in every room.*

She unfastened the shutters and pulled open the drapes. The Sun shined in and rousted the spider spirits sleeping in a maze of tattered cobwebs hanging from the ceiling. The light of day disturbed the tiny astral tics embedded in the dust. The hidden predators departed in haste and traveled to other destinations seeking new victims.

> *Golden streamers of light*
> *Made Sunny's house happy and bright.*

She opened the windows and the Wind blew in.

> *The Wind zipped and zapped and went on its way.*
> *It whirled and twirled without delay.*

The Wind bowed and greeted glorious Father Sun: "Hail to Thee, Lord of Light. Come dance with me!" The Sun and the Wind danced the jig in circles going from room to room.

Kriya laid sprigs of dried cedar and sage in a lustrous abalone shell. With the flick of a match, the leaves were alight, and began to smolder and purify the room. The Wind came to help, gently blowing the smudge into the crevices and corners, and the hiding places of the gremlets and their kin.

The aromatic smoke dissipated the cloud of oppression that had been weighing down on Tom and Kriya, keeping their minds in a haze. At last, Kriya could stand tall again and spread her wings. Finally, Tom and Kriya could see with clarity and envision a brighter future.

The Rules of the Gremlets

As the haze of negativity was dispelled by the aromatic vapors of the smudge, Mirabel felt safe to venture out from her rafter hideaway and find her way home to Tom and Kriya, and her warm and cozy bed in the closet. Before she left the retreat, she wanted to speak one more time with the Tiger master and seek his enlightened counsel.

Mirabel complained, "Those *darn* gremlets are troublemakers. Why don't they behave like the rest of us and be nice little gremlets? Why don't they just follow the rules?"

Mirabel was an obedient cat who did not like to make waves. Order and regularity made her feel safe. Princess was a free spirit who trusted her inner guidance, not knowing where it would lead her. She was an explorer cat who dared to venture into unknown lands, lured by the magic of discovering the miracles of life.

Tiger was wise. He felt connected to the Source within him. He was happy to share with Mirabel all that he knew and everything he had learned. He explained to her that gremlets and humans have different operating systems. He said, "They do not act like humans, or even like cats, because they belong to a different race of beings. Born and bred to be gremlets, they play by a different set of rules."

Mirabel said, "To all gremlets everywhere I say: *Grow up and be nice.*"

"They are not programmed to be nice the way you would like. They are locked into their programming and cannot change," Tiger explained.

"Well, I'm glad I am a cat and can decide how I want to be," Mirabel was grateful.

"Many humans do not recognize their divine good luck. They have the power of choice called *free will.* They can create their destiny. They can adapt and grow."

Mirabel was angry at the gremlets. "I find them annoying," she protested. "I want them to go away and leave me alone!"

"Happiness is the cure for what ails you," Tiger replied. "When you are feeling intense anger or depression, for example, they pick up your vibe with their psychic mood detectors. They sense your inner state and may try to latch onto you to feed off your emotional energy."

"I see," replied Mirabel. "They don't bother Princess because she is an optimist. They seek out Marshall and Malachi because they are discontent and angry at life. Being happy has practical value," she realized.

"If people around the world could be happy for just one day, the gremlets and their kin would die of starvation and humanity would be free at last!" Tiger was convinced.

Friends in Disguise

Mirabel wasn't ready to forgive the gremlets for being who they were. They were behaving the way they were designed to act, but that was not good enough for her. Again she complained, "This is the first place ever that I have met these spooky little critters, and I hope it will be the last!"

Tiger was thoughtful. "There is another way to look at things, a deeper way to see. The gremlets are not our enemies. They are friends in disguise. We can thank them for showing us the wounded places we need to heal, those places of brokenness that have not let in God's love."

Mirabel was earnest. "How do they show us what we need to heal?"

"They harass us by targeting our weaknesses. When we heal ourselves, they have a hard time finding an opening to hook into us. When we heal ourselves, they lose their power to manipulate us and trigger emotional reactions."

Mirabel understood. "When we recognize our weaknesses, we can transform them into strengths."

"Now you see it differently. You changed your point of view."

"I guess they are not such bad guys after all," Mirabel admitted.

"They become our teachers when we are willing to learn from our experiences with them," Tiger explained. "The Dark serves the Light in mysterious ways."

"I see. We need to look beneath the surface and not be fooled by appearances."

"Right on!" Tiger agreed. "They send us energies our bodies translate into emotions that we believe are our own. They project disturbing thoughts into our minds that masquerade as our own thoughts."

"I don't want to be outsmarted by their cleverness," Mirabel replied, swelling with feline pride. "How can I tell the difference between their thoughts and mine?"

Tiger answered, "It takes vigilance. It takes practice and self-awareness. Get to know your own mind; notice your moods and basic attitudes. When there is a down-shift in your energy, you may be under their influence. They thrive on your self-pity, depression, anger, hatred and fear."

"I will learn to pay attention," she resolved. "I don't want to be a victim. I want to be free!"

Good-bye, Dear Friend

Mirabel could sense Tiger's apprehension about his future path. "What is your next step going to be?" she asked with concern. They touched noses, as is customary among cats, and gazed deeply into each other's eyes.

"I am not ready to go back. I am not ready to move forward. I will remain here and meditate until the answer becomes clear," he replied.

"Will I see you again?" Mirabel wondered.

"I can't promise anything. Not at this point. Maybe yes. Maybe no."

Kitty tears ran down her furry cheeks as Mirabel looked lovingly at Tiger. "My dear friend," she said sweetly, "I am sad to say good-bye. I shall love you always and forever. I shall remember your wisdom and your grace." She bowed her head to honor her beloved friend and teacher. "May the Light always shine upon you."

Turning away from her longtime companion, she crept along the beam, carefully balancing herself, and then climbed down the post to enter the space between the walls. A faint light beckoned her forward as she approached the opening to the upstairs bathroom. Crawling out from under the claw-footed bathtub, she stealthily made her way down the hall. Finding the door to the attic room slightly ajar, she pushed it open with her paw, and went directly to the water bowl.

Now that Tiger was alone, he could reflect more deeply on the choice he was about to make. He knew he would be taking a risk by leaving the security of Tom and Kriya's love. Was he ready to leave the nest and venture out on his own?

He remembered his vow from long ago. As a young kitten, traumatized by watching an act of cruelty to his mother, he had resolved to create a world where people live in peace and harmony.

He prayed: "Dear God, please direct my every step. I choose to walk the path of peace, and to shine the Light of Love into the hearts of humanity and all creatures everywhere. Amen."

Welcome Home, Mirabel

Kriya's heart leapt with joy when she saw her beloved Mirabel drinking from the water bowl. Mirabel was glowing, her eyes shining. "Welcome home, Mirabel!" Kriya exclaimed with excitement. "You are my special kitty, dear to my heart. I love you so." As she opened a box of kibbles, she thought of Tiger. "Where is Tiger? He has not come back. Only yourself."

During Mirabel's time of retreat with Tiger, she became attuned to his psyche. She offered her interpretation of his intentions: "He hears a call and wants to see where it will lead him. To do this he needs to be free. He can no longer remain here and be with you. He loves you as always but feels destiny is calling."

Mirabel's report did not please Kriya. She tended to shut down when under duress, as when the Universe did not conform to her will. She was not ready to accept Tiger's choice and see his point of view. She took it to heart that her beloved Tiger did not return. She took it personally and blamed herself, as if she could control life, as if she were responsible for things beyond her grasp. She thought, *Am I giving the cats enough attention? I have been so preoccupied with helping Tom recover from his accident, maybe I ignored the cats without realizing it.*

Mirabel continued, "He hears the call, like Princess heard the call resounding in her heart that led her to venture forth to meet her teacher. Just because he is a cat doesn't mean he isn't capable of greatness. Everyone knows that cats can save the world."

Kriya philosophized, "I think we humans underestimate the abilities of cats, and our animal friends everywhere. Perhaps angels experience Earth by incarnating as cats, or as horses or eagles."

"Tiger is destined to become an animal star for the children of Earth," Mirabel imagined. "He is a good dancer with a natural sense of rhythm. He dances in step with the present moment. In my mind's eye, I can see him performing on stage, entertaining the troops of humankind."

Mirabel looked around. She sensed a shift in the energy. "Where are the gremlet twins, those nasty dudes Mister Red and his pal Mister Orange?" she asked.

"They are gone, give thanks."

"Hurray! Hurray!" Mirabel was overjoyed. "Did you yell at them and order them to leave? I don't think they would go willingly; they needed to be thrown out by force."

"Princess taught me the ancient art of smudging," explained Kriya. "I performed a ritual of purification using the smoke of aromatic herbs to cleanse the house of negativity."

Primed to enter the conversation, Princess jumped down from her favorite seat on the windowsill. She said, "The vapors of smoldering sage are akin to bug repellent for astral pests, causing them to flee." The white cat enjoyed sharing wisdom teachings from the Sisters of the Forest.

Mirabel was grateful. "At last I can relax!"

Princess described the amazing qualities of smudge. "It dissipates subtle energies that linger in a room. Thought-forms hover in the air after the thinker has left. Intense emotions leave a residue felt by empaths and sensitives, creating a mood or atmosphere. These energies settle in the woodwork, in cracks and crevices and dust. People whose minds churn in a raging sea of recycled thoughts and discontent find it difficult to let go of the past. Smudge clears away the thought-forms, like a cosmic reset button to the here-and-now."

Mirabel exclaimed, "A new day dawns for all of us free from the trouble-maker twins."

Sunny Returns

Slam! went the front door as the old house rocked upon its foundation. The china clinked and clattered in the kitchen cabinets and the paintings vibrated against the living room walls. The Wind whisked its way along and whished itself up the stairs. It zipped around the corner landing and zapped down the hallway right into Tom and Kriya's attic room. The windowpanes rattled as Princess sat at her lookout post, watching the world go by.

The Spirit of the Wind saluted the great white princess: "Hail, Royal Highness of CatLand!"

"What brings you hither?" she inquired of the Wind Spirit.

"I am the messenger of change. I bring you news of the moment. The lady of the house has returned. Adieu!"

Princess jumped onto the bed to get Kriya's attention. Her mistress was absorbed in writing a letter to a friend that she missed. "Prepare yourself," said Princess. "Sunny is back from her journey. It would be wise for you to go downstairs and welcome her home."

Kriya wanted to make a favorable impression on Sunny. She felt her survival depended on Sunny's whim. She had no money in the bank and no relatives to take them in along with all three cats. Like Tom, she needed rest and healing as her life force was depleted from struggling to survive.

She slipped on a pink floral dress that accentuated the curves in her slender figure. Kriya felt it was important to look attractive to Sunny, a seamstress with an eye for fashion. She brushed her hair, making it shine, taking her time. She was feeling anxious to greet Sunny and speak her truth to her. It was still a mystery why Sunny had not told her about her sons, nor given her instructions on how to treat them. At some point, she needed to confront her and ask her directly.

Kriya found her seated at her desk in the sewing room, opening the mail. Sunny looked up and smiled brightly, her brown eyes shining.

"Hello, Kriya! Good to see you."

"Hi, Sunny. Welcome home."

"Thank you."

"How was your healing journey to New Mexico?"

"It was fantastic! I learned the Indian ways, their respect for Nature and reverence for the Earth."

"Did you connect with Dancing Eagle, the medicine woman you were excited to meet?"

"Oh. Yes. She taught me how to communicate with the spirits of plants, that they might teach me how to extract their medicine. We foraged the hillsides gathering roots and seeds, and traveled by horseback from village to village to attend ceremonies attuned to the stars. I watched as she performed sacred rituals to drive away evil spirits that tormented the souls of her people."

Ah so! thought Kriya, *We could use those rituals here and now.*

Ding a ling! Ding a ling! The telephone rang and Sunny shot up from her desk to answer it. Kriya waited as Sunny chatted on and on.

Kriya was disappointed, as she had been mentally preparing for this moment, anticipating their conversation. She wanted to confront Sunny about the delinquent deeds of her socially defiant sons. What were Sunny's rules? What were her expectations? Her assumptions?

As she left the room, she heard Sunny laugh. "Yes, Auntie Opal. Tea on Tuesday," Sunny said and laughed again.

Hexagram 20

Kriya headed up the stairs and back to her attic sanctuary. Tom was seated at the table tossing copper pennies. Fascinated by *The Book of Changes,* more than ever he wanted to be flowing with the Tao. He thought, *I hope the I Ching can point us in the direction we need to go. We want to create a more promising future and we need to start from within.*

Tom looked up at Kriya as she closed the door behind her. He was writing down the results of his coin toss in a notepad he kept for that specific purpose: a coin toss log recording the date, the question, and the guidance that came through. He was serious about his studies of the wisdom masters of the East. Kriya sat down at the table across from him. "It didn't work out," she began, appearing sad and dejected as she reported on her encounter with Sunny. "My timing was off. Just as I was about to speak my truth and confront her, the telephone rang. Was the Universe listening?"

"It is best to wait until you can come from a calm center," he suggested. "Your anxiety could jinx the outcome. If you are experiencing fear, you are projecting an unsettling energy that she may sense and react to, no matter what you are saying, no matter how good your intentions."

"Maybe I'm not ready yet. I need to think things through," she responded.

"Take your time. Tune in. Sense when it is right for you. Wait until you feel comfortable within yourself and your confidence will shine. Sometimes, dear Kriya, you are so headstrong you set yourself up for disappointments. A little patience goes a long way."

"I don't know how to read Sunny," said Kriya. "Who is she anyway?"

"Her fantasies seem to work for her," Tom surmised. "She appears pleased with her life, happy as a lark, or perhaps she is an actress fooling even herself."

Kriya was critical, "I think she is irresponsible as a mother. She is too focused on herself."

"You are judging her," he observed.

"That is my opinion. Motherhood is the most important job on the planet. I stand up for women and their unacknowledged service to the world. What does Sunny stand for, I would like to know?"

"She just sits on the fence. That is the way I see it. Then she can go either way and doesn't have to commit. When you live in a dream-world, which way is up?" he wondered.

"We don't need to figure her out to find our way out. We can create a new reality for ourselves without ever knowing where she's at in her thinking or who she is," Kriya affirmed.

Tom admired his wife's spirit of inquiry and her dedication to the truth. He said, "I agree, we need to find out who *we* are, not who *she* is. When we get clear on what we really want, we can take our next step. Self-knowledge is our ticket out of here."

"Let's search our hearts and agree on a dream we can believe in. Our dream-vision will become our stepping stone to move from an undesired now to a chosen future," she said thoughtfully.

Kriya eyed his notebook and asked, "What is your reading for today, December 3, 1993?"

"Hexagram 20," he answered. "Kuan / Contemplation. It says, *To know where to go, we need to contemplate where we are.*"

Tea on Tuesday

Golden rays of morning light danced upon Kriya's pillow, then skipped across the room in pure delight. "Wake up, Kriya," urged Father Sun. The Lord of the Sky was shining the light of Heaven upon the Earth, awakening people to a new day.

The walls of the attic room vibrated from the bustle of activity in the kitchen below as Sunny hurried and scurried, preparing for the arrival of her guests. Auntie Opal, and her lady friends Patty Pearl and Ruby Red, had been invited for tea.

Like a robin in spring, Sunny flitted about in her garden greenhouse, picking fragrant blossoms and tossing them into the pockets of her apron. Artfully, she arranged bouquets of Mother Nature's marvelous creations, displaying them in vintage vases. On the dining room table, she laid out a white lace tablecloth, smoothing out the wrinkles and setting the vases at each end. As the centerpiece, she chose a golden swan, known for its sublime grace and elegant beauty.

The pleasant aroma of cinnamon and spices wafted from the oven. Sunny was baking teacakes, pastries and shortbread cookies. Kriya greeted her as she neatly folded the cloth napkins.

"Good morning, Sunny. What a beautiful day!"

"Good morning, Kriya. Nice to see you. The house looks great! You and Tom did a fine job. You are welcome to stay here as long as you like."

"Thank you," she replied. "We are grateful to have a place to stay."

The buzzer rang and Sunny put on her oven mitts to remove a tray of steaming hot apple turnovers. After the table was set and the pastries were cooling, she dusted her grandmother's Victrola and played a record of a string quartet to set the mood. As the violins sang sweetly and the cello wept, she let out a sigh of relief.

Ring! Ring! sounded the doorbell. Sunny graciously welcomed her guests.

"It is so lovely to see you again, my dear child," exclaimed Auntie Opal. She gave Sunny a big hug and handed her a box of heart-shaped chocolates. Ruby Red smiled and gave her a cranberry raisin fruitcake. Patty Pearl curtsied and offered a jar of homemade strawberry preserves. When all of the ladies were seated at the table, Sunny poured hot tea. "Cream and sugar, if you please," she offered her guests.

"How is life treating you?" they asked.

"Fine. Just fine."

"How are the boys doing in school?"

"Fine. Just fine."

"How is your sewing business?"

"Fine. Just fine," Sunny smiled. "Everything is perfect in my world. Thank you."

In the Name of Freedom

While Sunny was upstairs playing hostess, graciously serving tea to her elegant lady visitors, a party was underway down below in the rebels' den. Teenage ruffians from across the neighborhood—budding young gangsters and hoodlums in training—had gathered in the name of Freedom. These young rebels lived outside the law and beyond the rules and parameters of society without a moral compass to guide them. They harvested forbidden fruit picked only by sinners. In the minds of the misfits:

We disagree with society.
We can be who we want to be.

Young rebels became anarchists when they undermined the order of the day. Freedom without conscience was a threat to one and all. They belonged to a threatening faction of malcontents intent on eroding the moral foundation of mainstream America.

The energy in the house had down-shifted after Sunny returned home. In the shadow of her presence, the unholy gremlet twins returned to their accustomed haunts. Their psychic radar was mood sensitive, and Sunny's morbid imagination drew them in. The venom of her unconscious found release in the pathos of her paintings. Art was an escape valve that allowed her to function within the ballpark of normalcy. The art museum was the breeding ground for the vibe of melancholy that pervaded her house.

While fleeing the repellant aromas of the smudge, the gremlets had traversed the astral landscape and arrived at their provincial home of Gremletville. Meeting with their next of kin, they sought out reinforcements to join their assault on impressionable minds. (Gremlets have big families because there is more power in numbers.) Volunteers followed after them, uncles and cousins, who returned en masse to Sunny's house. As leaders of the troops, Alderon and Algenon gave orders to their underlings: Adon, Aldon, Andon, Alcidon and Aldicon. They grinned with devilish delight as they projected nasty thoughts into the minds of the unsuspecting young rebels.

Each gremlet chose a victim, straddling the boys' shoulders and shouting unseemly exhortations in their ears.

> *The boys puffed on cigars and acted tough.*
> *They spit and cursed, appearing gruff.*
> *They drank hard liquor, more than enough.*

Agents of darkness employ strategies of deception to lure truth seekers off the path. Untrained psychics can be fooled when malevolent spirits appear to them disguised as angels, or Jesus, or some great god from beyond.

The Power of the Media

The eerie feeling pervading the household evoked an air of apprehension that overshadowed the lives of Tom and Kriya. Only Princess, the intrepid feline, seemed unruffled by the undercurrents of evil circulating like cold drafts. Kriya's nerves were on edge. Tom was ill at ease. Day and night, he was seeking a resolution to their dilemma. "How is your detective work coming along?" he inquired of his wife.

"It's not," she replied. "I think I need to talk to the boys directly to get my answers. Studying Sunny's paintings could lead me on a wild goose chase. How would I verify my conclusions? How would I know?"

"You might be right, but if I were you, I would employ my empathy and intuition to sense the emotions evoked by her paintings. There is more to this than meets the eye."

"Well, okay, I see your point. I'll take another look and see what I see."

Preparing herself for the task ahead, Kriya took out the notepad she used to record her observations and impressions. Upon entering the museum, she immediately was drawn to the portrait of Uncle Daniel. Searchingly she looked into his eyes, attempting to discern his inner essence.

Daniel felt the intensity of her gaze and stepped out of the painting to converse with her. This time Kriya feared not, as her previous encounter had convinced her of his trustworthiness.

"What is disturbing you, young lady?"

Kriya was taken aback. *How does he know I am disturbed?* she wondered. *I came here on a detective mission, not looking for a psychoanalyst. But maybe I'll tell him anyway just to see what he says.* "Sunny's boys Marshall and Malachi spend countless hours riveted to the television set, transfixed by the hypnotic power of the electronic media. Hanging out around the TV are these little red and orange spirit critters that become emboldened when violent programming is turned on. They shout obscenities into the boys' ears and goad them to commit acts of aggression. I saw them with my own eyes. It is for real."

"There is a tie-in between the media and the spirit entities that benefit. They are in cahoots," he claimed.

"Sunny said you were given high security clearance by military intelligence. What did you learn?"

Daniel looked serious as he reflected on Kriya's question. He replied, "The Controllers of the mainstream media are ardent students of the human psyche. They spy on us, they monitor us, amassing data to be used to manipulate our motivations and behaviors. The more they know about us, the better they can control us. They are designing a psychological road map delineating how humans operate, and how to utilize our weaknesses.

"The plan is to keep humanity operating at a low frequency that limits perception. When people reach a more expanded awareness, they will see through the veils of deceit. Those in the know who expose these nefarious schemes are deemed as threats to the power elite and condemned as traitors and criminals. The shadow government employs covert means to assassinate truth-tellers like me," he reported from first-hand experience.

"The more aware we become, the less we can be controlled," Kriya agreed. "Our power lies in our consciousness."

"The corporate media promotes the agenda of the Controllers," he continued. "The people are persuaded to buy into the official version of reality as broadcast by the media and fabricated by the Controllers. The people are deceived into believing their seductive lies. The truth has no value. Only perception counts.

"Science fiction writers and film makers prepare the public to accept the future scenarios they intend to perpetrate. In contrast, men of conscience have written exposés of the totalitarian agenda to warn the people of impending suppression if 'the many' give up their power to 'the few'— *Brave New World* is an example, and *Nineteen Eighty-Four*."

"Who are these so-called Controllers you are telling me about?" Kriya wanted to know what he knew.

"There is a hierarchy of control, a pyramid structure of command, with the Controllers at the very top. They are invisible to us because they exist in a dimension beyond the range of human sight. They don't have a conscience like we do, or emotional capabilities such as empathy and compassion. The Controllers hold the reins of power for the owners of the mainstream media, the CEOs of transnational corporations, the medical industry, governments and central banks. Their puppets are akin to psychopaths because they are destroying the biosphere of our planet and instigate war for profit without concern for the human cost.

"They want to close the human heart and create a race of slave automatons callous to the suffering of others," he explained. "One tactic is to desensitize people to the pain of others by replaying film clips of horrid deeds. These ghastly events can seem almost normal after we see them portrayed again and again."

"Where is the public protest against the horrors of war? Where is the moral outcry against injustice and genocide?" Kriya questioned the people's perspective.

He replied, "Countless people of heart have dedicated their lives to ending war and creating a peaceful world. Millions of books have been written deprecating war and promoting global peace and brotherhood. Yet war rages on and the toll of suffering mounts. To eradicate the scourge of war, we need to pull it out by the roots. We need to expose the fear agenda that is poisoning the hearts of the people."

"Public education is set up to indoctrinate children to obey authority and to inculcate national loyalty," Kriya believed. "They are taught that power lies outside of themselves."

Daniel agreed, "The Controllers want us to give them our power. Their success depends on our subconscious consent." He continued, "The System molds young men into good soldiers to fight as pawns in wars planned by the Controllers. Boys are raised to act tough and suppress their emotional nature. Boot camp is designed to break the will of the soldier. The ritual of war offers a feast for the energy predators that feed off human suffering."

"How do you know what you know?" Kriya asked. "Where did you learn all of this stuff?" she was curious.

"I hold a degree in societal engineering from the University of the Airwaves. At UA I studied the mind control technologies employed by the media. After graduating, the government offered me a top-notch position in a secret program run by the Department of Defense. In our laboratories, we experimented on people using frequencies and monitored their reactions."

"How so?" Kriya wondered.

"The frequency range of human brainwaves is three to thirty cycles per second on the electromagnetic spectrum. We scanned the brainwaves of an individual and mimicked them with simulated frequencies until the person's brain became entrained. The biological emissions of the psyche were synchronized with the man-made frequencies. Gradually, we altered the frequencies of our broadcast and the person's brainwaves followed suit.

"We were preparing to test specific frequencies on segments of the population. Once we could replicate the energy dynamics of thoughts and emotions, we wanted to motivate desired behaviors. Crowd control is an example—keeping the public sedated. And the other extreme—inciting riots and creating mayhem. Electromagnetic frequencies were an invisible weapon in the arsenal of the psychopaths who sought to control humanity.

"I quit when I finally realized what they were up to. Behind their research lay malicious intentions—an assault on the human psyche. I needed to stand in my integrity. After that, I landed a job as a sound technician at Majestic Studios. I am a suspicious observer, so I snooped around when the security was lax. I began to catch on to their secret programs hidden behind the façade of legitimacy. Let me show you."

"Show me what?"

"Just come with me and step inside the painting. It isn't the way it looks. The oil and canvas are just a front. We'll go through a portal that takes us to Hollywood and Command Central of mind control operations."

"Well, I don't want to get stuck in the painting. And Hollywood is hundreds of miles away." Kriya hesitated. She needed to consult her intuition.

Command Central

Kriya paused for a moment as she tuned in and accessed her inner guidance. A leap of faith was required to step into the unknown. She thought, *How much am I willing to risk to uncover the truth?* Her heart pounding, she took a deep breath and plunged into the painting.

Daniel led the way. He took her hand, and off they went on their daring venture. They had landed in a modern world, an electronic wonderland. They strolled through stands of illumined trees in a magnificent electronic forest. Growing wild amidst the electric trees were living trees soaring skyward, an integrated landscape of man-made and living creations.

Upon reaching the crest of a hill, a vast vista opened up before them. Covering the plains below them was a gridwork of vibration generators. Rotating corkscrews of glowing neon lights, green and red and cobalt blue, streamed waves of primal energy. Daniel explained, "These spinning tubes of light generate power from One Source energy. You see, this world has achieved the ultimate balance between nature and technology. It is a lesson humanity has yet to learn."

He approached a rock-strewn slope on the far side of the power station. One after another, he overturned each moss-covered rock and probed the ground underneath with his hand, searching for the opening he knew was there. "I am looking for the portal to Hollywood. We shall descend through an underground tunnel leading to the film studio where I worked years ago."

Daniel spotted a slab of slate, appearing like a manhole cover. With all his might, he pried it loose and pushed it to one side. "I found it!" he exclaimed. "This is the way." Leaning over the edge of the portal, he looked down, down, down into the bowels of the Earth. "I'll go first," he shouted. "Just follow me." He slid down a chute inside a tunnel that twisted and turned this way and that way, without rhyme or reason. He had no control except over his mind.

Kriya's turn was next. Hesitating at the top of the chute, she wondered: *Does Daniel know where he is going? Can I trust him to lead the way?* Once again her commitment to discover the truth was being tested. *I am not backing down out of fear,* she was resolute.

She prayed for angelic protection, took a deep breath, and jumped into the portal. She closed her eyes to protect them from bits of stone falling off the walls of the subterranean tunnel. She felt the energy shifting as the chute descended and spiraled around.

In no time they emerged through a cloaked opening covered by a latticework of fallen branches. Pushing her way through to the light of day, Kriya climbed onto solid land, grateful for her safe arrival. She dusted the dirt off her clothes, smoothed down her hair, and mentally prepared herself for anything and everything. Daniel looked around. He hoped more than ever that they had jumped into the right portal. Where were they?

Sweet tropical scents tantalized the senses. They found themselves in a lovely oriental garden, lush with bamboo, plum, and lotus. This verdant mini-paradise fronted the entrance gate to Majestic Studios, their intended destination. Fortune smiled on Dan and Kriya, as the guard on duty recognized the former employee, and he waved them forward without requesting ID for security clearance.

"Wait a minute!" exclaimed Kriya, "Break time!" They sat down on a wooden bench in the courtyard inside the confines. "That guard saw you!" she confronted him. "Are you a ghost, or a soul presence, or what? I thought I was able see you because I am clairvoyant. How did the guard see you?"

"I decide who sees me and who doesn't. I am a shaman with psychic powers. When I need a body, I create one at will. I didn't really die when they killed me. My spirit lives on."

"We live forever. It is just the body that dies," she believed.

Before them was a vast array of buildings set at angles to one another, a non-linear reality. An ominous black obelisk stood in the center of the complex, towering above the executive offices, laboratories, and data storage facilities. The antenna apparatus on the roof of the obelisk housed frequency transmitters aimed at target populations for experimentation. Military police were not needed because frequency control kept the public in line with the prevailing program. Those who emanated higher consciousness vibrated above the controlling frequencies and escaped the clutches of the propaganda machine.

Kriya looked up and saw the antennae on the roof begin to rotate and transmit in all directions. "The signals being broadcast are concocted in the psychic labs," said Daniel. "They can drive people to commit suicide, or incite them to perpetrate heinous crimes that strike fear into the hearts of the people.

"The secret plan is to prey on people's addictive tendencies, weakening their will and undermining their personal power. Electronic stimulation can elicit an endorphin response, creating a high that gets people hooked. Soon the face of the planet will be pockmarked by millions of cell phone towers transmitting frequencies adverse to health and happiness. The lure of technology is bait to program young people to meld their minds with electronic devices. Heed this warning: If we don't watch out, people will forfeit their essential human nature to become akin to robots and androids that obey commands."

Kriya thought, *That seems far-fetched. Is this guy on the level?* She countered, "I don't believe you. We as a species are smarter than that. We won't let it happen."

"Forewarned is forearmed. We need to be vigilant or we will lose control over our minds and our lives." Daniel was dead serious.

They had entered the clandestine headquarters of Command Central, the strategic planning center of mind control operations. Under the guise of Majestic Studios of Hollywood fame, mind control programs were developed to keep the public complacent, compliant, and obedient.

Walking through a revolving glass door, they stepped into the lobby of the obelisk. The receptionist at the front desk was absorbed in a self-indulgent moment of narcissism, admiring her ravishing beauty in a gilded vanity mirror and smiling with pleasure at her reflection. They scurried past the receptionist and passed through a turnstile into the inner sanctum. Daniel pushed a sequence of buttons on a keypad by a steel door, and they unobtrusively entered Room One, careful not to disturb the programming specialists focused on their monitors. He whispered, "Majestic Studios proudly produces the latest and the greatest, the most state-of-the-art mind control technologies praised by shadow governments around the world."

As quietly as they entered, Daniel and Kriya slipped out of Room One to the elevator station across the hall. "We are going to the top," Daniel announced. "We are going all the way up." During their ascent, he filled Kriya in on some of the history: "After World War II, our military intelligence arranged for ex-Nazi scientists who had knowledge of mind control to come to the US and begin a programming center here. This research has been going on for decades—how to harness the powers of the subconscious mind to enslave the population. The battleground for psychic warfare lies within the hearts and minds of the people."

They stepped out of the elevator and walked onto a balcony overlooking the entire complex. Kriya felt ill at ease being exposed to the intense electromagnetic field. She thought, *This place is buzzing. I don't want to be zapped.*

"I am going back inside," she announced abruptly and retreated into the interior of the obelisk. Ahead of her, she saw a lounge area facing a window with a commanding view. Daniel sat down next to her, eager to continue his exposé: "The Controllers establish the framework of the official reality they want to implement. The Ministry of Information follows suit and orders the media syndicates to suppress information that does not conform to the authorized worldview. Control of perception—that is the key to subjugating the masses. Command Central formulates the social engineering programs that trick people into agreeing on a reality that does not exist."

"How can frequency control the mind?" she asked.

"Television watching induces a trance-like state. Brainwave activity is slowed down to the theta frequency, and the critical mind is bypassed. Theta frequency is the ideal medium for programming the subconscious, instilling beliefs and attitudes useful to those in control," he explained.

"The test of our time is to know what is real," he continued. "The human race stands dazed in the crossfire of competing belief systems vying for followers."

"The brave of heart need to take a stand and speak the truth," said Kriya. "People power can win the day if we all unite as one."

"The power of collective intention can turn the tide for Good," Daniel agreed.

"I hope we don't turn into a race of mindless automatons," Kriya shuddered at the thought and wondered: *How do we know where our thoughts are coming from? Who owns our minds? The media technocrats and propaganda wizards surreptitiously put ideas in our minds just like the gremlets do.*

The Sword of Truth

Tom sat in the chair by the window reflecting on the unforeseen chain of events that brought them to Sunny's house. He spent his alone-time immersed in introspection, searching his soul for guidance and insight. In his mind, he replayed past scenarios, questioning his choices and the motivation behind them.

He opened the attic window to take a breath of fresh air. Princess was sitting at her accustomed lookout post on the windowsill. The chirrup of a little bird had captured her attention. On hearing the sweet melodies of birdsong, she perked up her ears and poked her head out the window. In an instant, she was standing on the outside ledge, and with a bounding leap, she landed on the outstretched branch of a grizzled old oak. Down she climbed the sturdy trunk until she felt the comforting turf of Mother Earth beneath her feet.

The sun had set and the full moon bathed the town and surrounding countryside in a resplendent silver glow. She remembered the teachings of the Violet Sister in the grove of Grandmother trees. "Seek out a place in the woods where the energy is strong," she had instructed Princess. "Draw in the Earth energy as a source of your power."

Could Princess reclaim her psychic abilities from long ago? During the time of King Arthur, she was the cat companion of Merlin, the renowned magician and sage of his day. Through their telepathic connection, she absorbed his knowledge of sorcery and became adept at casting spells and performing rituals and ceremonies.

Traversing the neighborhood of old mansions and fine houses, she headed for an overgrown field away from the glare of streetlights and the drone of traffic. Finding her way through the underbrush, she came upon a trail that led her deep into the forest. Sensing the subtle shifts in the energy around her, she was being guided to find her place of power. Venturing along the moonlit trail, she began to climb and wind her way around the side of a mountain. As the pink rays of dawn tinted the emerging landscape, Princess arrived at her destination. She stood on a rocky promontory and felt the energy of Mother Earth surging through her paws. She felt her power returning. Now was the time.

A flash of lightning streaked across the sky. As the thunder roared, a brilliant orb of light descended from the Heavens and assumed the form of a mighty angel. Clad in the armor of battle, He wore a peaked helmet of gold and brandished a double-edged sword spouting a sacred blue flame. "I am Archangel Michael, warrior Angel of the Light," He introduced himself. "The Violet Sister has called on Me to assist you at this moment of claiming your power. From afar, she lovingly watches over you and monitors your progress on your path."

Princess was overjoyed. "Thank You, bright Angel" she exclaimed. "I am ready for the next step."

"I offer you the Sword of Truth for your safety and protection. It is a spiritual weapon to cut through lies and illusion. Those who use the Sword amplify the vibration of Truth in the world."

With courage in her heart, Princess proudly unsheathed the Sword and imagined aiming it at the naughty spirits. "Grizwald: Beware!" she shouted. "Alderon and Algenon, your time has come!"

Michael explained, "As more and more people learn to wield the Sword, the moral climate of society will change. Let the Light of Truth bring clarity to arguments and understanding to adversaries. Shine the Light of Truth into the

Halls of Justice when testimony is given and verdicts are deliberated. Let It ignite the pen of the journalist to write with integrity and fairness. Shine It into the hearts of world leaders that they may be guided by wisdom and act with compassion."

Princess thanked Archangel Michael. She had a weapon of the Light at her disposal now to protect her cat family and her human family. She was grateful to the Universe for divine intervention.

Brother against Brother

It was past the midnight hour when Kriya emerged from the life-sized painting and stepped into the art museum. The onset of reality sent her reeling. *Where am I? I remember. Back to where I came from.* She sat on the floor facing Daniel's portrait, trying to get a grip on herself after a plunge into another reality. Her mind was turned on, in high gear, evaluating Daniel's claims to the unadulterated truth. *How do I know what is true?* she asked her higher mind.

His genuineness was clear to her. He felt trustworthy at heart. *I must help this man!* she concluded. *I feel responsible more than ever to take a stand for truth and freedom. I will honor his request and write the book he is suggesting. I will shine light on the darkness so the truth can be known.* She stood up and paced back and forth, reflecting, *Evil is empowered when people deny its existence. It's not hard to see when you are willing to look.*

A burst of machinegun fire jolted her attention back to the here-and-now. She sensed it was coming from the TV nook, where Marshall and Malachi sat slouching on the couch drinking beer, enthralled by their addiction to intense emotions elicited by the Hollywood script. Alderon was seated on Marshall's left shoulder. Algenon was sitting on Malachi's right shoulder. They wielded their greatest power when the teens sat spellbound in front of the television set.

Alderon clasped a plastic megaphone and pointed the cone at Marshall's ear, *Go get Malachi! Punch him out!* Then he flashed into Marshall's mind a visual image of him jumping onto his younger brother, a picture so compelling that Marshall pounced and Malachi fell to the ground.

Kriya watched from the sidelines, not feeling physically strong enough to interfere, terrified, panicking, not knowing what to do. To her relief, the fight was soon over. She ran upstairs to the sanctuary of their attic room, and to the protection of Tom's love.

House Rules

Watching Marshall attack his brother left Kriya shaken. She lay in bed, hyped up and unable to fall sleep. Her restless mind was conjuring up possible solutions for a way out of their predicament. She knew it was time to confront Sunny; she wanted clear answers. What were Sunny's expectations? Violence at her doorstep—what was going on?

The next morning, Kriya summoned her courage. As she slowly and deliberately walked down the three flights of stairs to the sewing room below, she rehearsed in her mind the much-anticipated conversation. *What kind of mood will Sunny be in today?* she wondered. *I must be strong,* she convinced herself.

The Lady of the House was standing at her ironing board softly singing a Native song she learned from Dancing Eagle. Sunny was wearing a flowing yellow dress with a matching yellow bow in her hair. The iron moved rhythmically back and forth, smoothing out the wrinkles of a long floral skirt.

"Hi, Sunny," Kriya began. "Good morning to you!"

"Oh, hello. You're up early, aren't you?"

"I know. I didn't sleep much last night. Marshall and Malachi were fighting. It scared me. What do you expect Tom and me to do?

She smiled, "Oh, boys will be boys," she casually remarked, dismissing Kriya's concern. Then she sang her theme song:

That's the way boys are.
That's the way it is.
That's the way I see it.
That's the way it is.

Kriya persisted. "What are the rules of your house?" she asked. Sunny sang her version of *House Rules*:

In my house, we play "Let's pretend."
Speak not the truth since it will offend.
Don't disturb my fantasy
With your version of reality.

Oh, I get it, Kriya thought. *Sunny and I don't share the same reality. Even if I knew what her rules were, would they apply to the Universe that I live in? Our thinking is worlds apart.* Kriya offered Sunny her perspective:

Everyone has their unique point of view.
Don't expect me to think like you.

She thought, *Sunny wants us to play the game of life by her rules, even though she never explained what they actually were. She just assumed we knew how to play her game her way and would join her in her dream-world. I guess we were supposed to pick up on it with some kind of mental osmosis.*

A Splendid Synchronicity

Kriya needed alone-time. She was mulling over her escapade with Uncle Daniel. *I must tell the world: Heed this warning. We are headed toward a totalitarian state if we don't take back our power and stand up for democracy.*

She stepped outside for a breath of fresh air. Sometimes a long walk would restore her sense of balance and mental clarity. She wandered up one street and down the next, her mind churning. *I must take responsibility for getting the word out. Uncle Daniel came into my life for a reason. Our meeting was meant to be.*

She entered a neighborhood of well-kept homes guarded by mighty oaks, their strong limbs providing a protective presence for the residents. Her imagination lured her in, and she found herself wondering: *Who lives in these houses? Are they more worthy or deserving than I am?*

Kriya turned a corner and came upon a narrow lane bordering a field overgrown with tall grasses and prickly bushes. She felt an energy pulling her forward and headed for a fork in the road where she spotted a deer path leading into the forest. *I must follow this trail*, her intuition spoke clearly. The sun was high in the sky; she had time to explore.

She followed the trail with no destination in mind. It felt good to be carefree for this moment and forget her struggle for survival. The realm of Nature was healing for her soul and set her mind at ease. In the quiet of contemplation she received a mental message from her beloved feline friend. "Greetings, Kriya. I am here!" *Lo and behold!* Princess was approaching from farther up the trail. Her green eyes glowing, she radiated an inner light.

Kriya was delighted beyond measure, abounding with joy at the sight of her dear and precious kitty. Since last night she had been worried when she realized that Princess was gone. She felt relieved that her little darling was safe and sound and had stayed out of harm's way.

Princess was happy to see Kriya. She was excited. "I spoke with an angel," she reported telepathically to Kriya.

"What did he say?"

"He said, 'I am Archangel Michael, warrior Angel of the Light. I am offering the Sword of Truth to everyone who wants to hold the Light for the world.'"

Kriya lovingly wrapped her arms around Princess and held her against her chest, carrying her back to 879 South Montrose Avenue. Entering their room, she poured a bowl of kibbles and sat down next to Tom. He smiled at his beloved. He was having a good day. "I have two amazing stories to tell you," she exclaimed.

"Number One?"

"Divine Synchronicity. I felt guided to follow a trail into the woods, and Princess crossed my path. My lesson is to trust the Universe. I need to let go more. There is a plan for Good at work in our lives even when the situation appears negative. The gift of difficult times is the lessons that show us the way."

Are You Brainwashed?

W hat is the other amazing thing that happened? I am
ready to hear Number Two."

"Uncle Daniel invited me to step into his portrait,"
she replied.

"And you accepted his invitation?"

"Yes. He convinced me to go with him. The paint and
canvas are just a façade. There are many worlds beyond what
meets the eye."

"Where did he take you?" he wondered.

"We went to a secret location in the foothills of
Hollywood. We walked through a gate opening into a vast
complex of offices, laboratories, and data storage facilities. To
the untrained eye, it appeared to be Majestic Studios, but
actually we had entered Command Central of mind control
operations. Looming over the scene was a mysterious black
obelisk with an antenna tower on the roof broadcasting in all
directions—transmitting frequencies to entrain people's
brainwaves, like a kind of electronic telepathy."

"Were you dreaming?" Tom was skeptical.

"No, I was fully awake, just like I am now."

"So, are you brainwashed? Like everyone else?" he teased
her.

"That won't happen to me!" She was fired up.

"Are you immune? Are you above it all?"

"I didn't say that! I got zapped by the EMF emitted from
the antenna tower. It sent me reeling. But I am okay now; I
shook it off."

"I think there is mind control everywhere," he theorized, "just that we aren't trained to recognize it as such. Even the words of our language create a trance in the way we see reality."

"Everyone wants us to think like them and abdicate our point of view. Diversity is what makes the world go round," she philosophized.

"Do you mean the world would stop spinning on its axis if we all thought the same?"

"Don't worry. That is not going to happen any time soon," she was convinced.

Meant to Be

I've been thinking." Tom closed the book he had been reading and looked at Kriya.

"When are you not thinking?" she remarked facetiously. "You are preoccupied with your inward journey."

"After months of soul searching," he began, "I have reached the conclusion that it is all *meant to be*. There are currents of destiny propelling us forward. Cosmic forces influence our lives and motivate us to act. Since the Big Bang at the Beginning, the Universe has been unfolding automatically."

"We live on a free will planet," she shared her point of view. "It is our job as humans to create. Everything we see around us first existed in the realm of thought."

"Everything we are creating was meant to be. That is how I see it. Our choices have been already made, then we become aware of them and claim them as our own. The Universe is acting through us, even when we experience being in control. It is a paradox, you see."

"How do you know?"

"Like a flash of insight, it dawned on me while I was meditating: When we perceive reality through the eye of the mind, we believe we are separate. Free will is personal will; it is an expression of the individual self. When we see through the eye of the heart, we perceive the unity of all things. The mundane is transformed into the sacred. Our personal will dissolves and we become instruments of the divine. We surrender and flow with the Tao, the universal will."

"I believe it is my path to learn to create and manifest," she replied. "I will surrender when the time is ripe."

The Power of Denial

Tom was not attached to being right. He was open to hearing points of view different from his own. *Maybe Kriya has something to teach me,* he was thinking. *I will look at life from her point of view.* He was willing to try on her way of thinking and to consider her perspective on the use of free will. He asked Kriya, "What did Uncle Daniel tell you?"

"He wants to warn us that our free will is being compromised. Little by little, it is being eroded away as the subversive programs become more sophisticated. He says people need to take responsibility for the contents of their minds. The culture of denial that pervades societal thinking hampers the free exercise of the will," she reported.

"How so?"

"Because people are shutting out information they need to make wise choices. They are not seeing the whole picture. They are looking through a distorted lens," she replied.

"Daniel is concerned that censorship is becoming rampant. We need to make choices with an open mind and we want facts that are reliable. It is critical we have access to a full spectrum of information before exercising our power of choice in the voting booth. When people are manipulated by the media, they make choices contrary to their best interest. Collective choices based on fear are a clear and present danger to our survival as a species."

Tom was thoughtful. "We need to step up to the plate and become conscious citizens of Planet Earth."

"We have yet to learn to take responsibility for our choices and the suffering we are unleashing on future generations. Our thoughts create ripples cascading down the stream of time," she believed.

"Feeling emotion is an essential component of living a human life," Tom offered his perspective.

"Suppressing our feelings can create dire consequences," she replied. "Emotions are our inner guidance system. They provide information the will needs for the process of making choices. Daniel is worried. The power of denial is so pervasive on our planet it is holding back the Light."

Call on Jesus

Kriya poured herself a glass of water and another one for Tom. She was grateful her husband could see what she saw and did not try to discredit Uncle Daniel. She thought Daniel was the real deal, that he was legit. She had faith in his integrity and believed the info she reported to Tom was trustworthy.

"What are you wanting now, Kriya?" he asked his wife.

She stood up and walked over to the window, then turned around and looked at him. "I want to feel safe. The spirit critters in this house give me the creeps. I want the gremlets to leave us alone, to stop bothering the cats and trying to manipulate Marshall and Malachi. Tom, you are a student of divinity. What have you learned?"

Tom remembered passages from the New Testament. "Jesus cast out demons. He was a healer who performed miracles of grace, freeing the possessed from tormenting spirits. There is inherent power in saying 'In the name of Jesus Christ.' If the spirits in this house try to mess with me, I will call on Jesus and declare: 'In the name of Jesus Christ, I command all negative entities to leave me now forever!'"

She applauded. "Right on! Way to go!"

Tom was curious, "Are they really as prevalent as you make out?"

"I suspect their interference is more commonplace than we realize," she reckoned, "just that we aren't taught how to recognize it happening in our own lives. Most people have no training in psychic protection, and how to free themselves from entities."

"Nobody talks about this stuff. At least no one I know," he said.

"Well, Uncle Daniel had a lot to say," she was sure of it. "He taught me how these malicious spirits operate. Our negative emotions transmit frequencies that attract them like magnets. For example, if we are already angry, they may create situations to inflame our anger. Our fear attracts spirits that fuel our fear. They foment emotional turmoil to feed off the chemicals produced by our reactions, hormones like testosterone for anger, cortisol and adrenalin for fear."

"Just because we have a few weird thoughts, does that mean our minds are being invaded?" he questioned her.

"Of course not. Our thoughts, most likely, are expressions of our core beliefs. Or our wounded inner child may be crying to be heard. Perhaps our guardian angels are sending us messages that register as thoughts. It takes practice to identify the negative tone and vibe of invasive thoughts apart from our own thought stream. We need to self-monitor and cultivate our discernment.

"Until we free ourselves from the grip of malevolent spirits, war, conflict, and destruction will continue on our planet," she attested. "Our suffering makes them tick. We cut off their sustenance when we experience inner peace, happiness and joy."

Picnic in the Park

Since you're hot on the trail of truth, why don't you take a closer look at the evidence? I mean, my dear detective, the boys—Marshall and Malachi. I suggest you talk to them directly and find out what they are really thinking," Tom advised.

"I already know that," she answered. "I need to access the power within me to come from a place of strength rather than fear when I face these angry young men. My father was an angry man and my cells still hold the trauma of abuse."

Kriya came up with a plan to make peace with the boys. "Maybe they would behave differently if I took them out into Nature, away from the virtual jungle with its addictions and delusions. I'll invite them for an afternoon picnic in the park. I'll make lemonade and sandwiches and bake chocolate chip cookies."

Marshall scoffed at the idea. He was plugged into the electronic reality, which was no more real, of course, than the dream-world that Sunny invented with her mind. Malachi, however, was quick to agree, in part because he wanted to escape his domineering older brother, get away from the ridicule and hurtful jabs, and find out who he was on his own terms.

After lunch, Kriya and Malachi set off for Rocky Mountain Lookout, hiking up a trail winding towards the summit. Malachi huffed and puffed as he plodded along, making a sincere effort to keep up. They sat down on a rough-hewn bench overlooking an expansive valley with the town of Meridian appearing through the distant haze.

Kriya's plan was to connect heart to heart with young Malachi. She dared to conjure up the courage to meet him as an equal and as a friend. She had envisioned them being honest with each other and connecting on a deep level. Away from the shadow of his overbearing older sibling, he appeared to be more sensitive and compliant.

"How is life for you?" she began the conversation.

"Life is not fair. There is no justice in the world. Not for me, not for anyone."

"I guess humanity has to grow up," she replied. "We need to treat each other better."

"Well, I certainly wasn't treated right. My dad beat me and my mom. She escaped into her imagination to avoid the anguish of his brutality. I was little and could not escape."

"What do you want now?" she asked him.

"I want to be free to experiment with life, to live outside the boundaries of other people's realities. Society tries to control me, but I rebel. The rules of society are like shackles holding me back. I want to make my own rules and live as I please:

I don't care what people think or say,
I do what I want, and I get my own way.

"We see the world through our own unique lens," Kriya responded. "There is no right or wrong way to live."

"I think my anger drives me to fight with life. I'll never be satisfied, because life is the enemy," he was convinced.

"When you look at life through the lens of anger, you see the world as a hostile place, with potential threats lurking around the corner. Is that what you want, Malachi?"

"I like being angry and upsetting the applecart. It's fun to watch people squirm. Peace is for wimps and sissies, not for rebels like me."

"I was angry when I was your age," Kriya remembered. "I blamed the world for my unhappiness. I saw the world through the lens of my emotional pain. Now those days are behind me. My life has turned around. And so can yours!"

The Deck of Life

Tom gazed out the window, daydreaming. Kriya sat down beside him. "Now it's your turn," she declared. "See if you can forge a friendship with Marshall and turn him towards the Light."

"I need to forgive him for his animosity. Then I can approach him with an open mind," he replied. Tom recalibrated his attitude as he sat in meditation. He remembered Kriya's wise counsel:

> *Everyone has their unique point of view.*
> *Don't expect them to think like you.*

He thought, *I must accept him for who he is. That is my mental starting place before I begin our conversation.*

After the boys returned home from school that day, Tom mustered up his courage and headed down the hall. He was able to maneuver freely now without dependency on crutches. When Marshall answered the knock on the door to his room, a startled look flashed in his eyes as he came face to face with Tom. Quickly he regained composure and projected his tough guy image. He morphed into Mr. Macho when his security felt threatened.

"What's up?" Marshall was suspicious.

"I have a music video that is right up your alley: *Days of Defiance* by the Oxymorons." This was Marshall's unparalleled favorite band, the unrivaled masters of the absurd. His face lit up and he opened the door wider, inviting Tom to enter his domain. As the teen accepted this offering of simpatico, a channel of communion began to open between former adversaries.

The room was in total disarray. Shiny silver candy wrappers, bottle caps, videos and magazines were scattered helter-skelter across the floor. Posters of rock stars exuding charisma and motorcycle queens on parade covered the walls. A row of green Coke bottles lined the windowsill.

Marshall sat down cross-legged on the floor and started shuffling a deck of Tarot cards. He split the deck in two and shuffled again, then laid out a spread of three cards in a row. Tom sat down on the floor to be on the same level as Marshall, sitting not too close, not too far away. As an aficionado of divination, he understood the synchronistic nature of card readings.

"What do you want to know?" Tom inquired.

"Who is to blame? Whose fault is it? Who is responsible?" Marshall was angry.

"Everyone is responsible, whether they know it or not. We have no one to blame but ourselves," Tom surmised.

"Well then, I say everyone is at fault. Society is to blame. The deck of life is stacked against me. I don't have a chance," lamented Marshall.

"Your future is before you. There is plenty of time to set things on track," Tom encouraged.

"The world is wrong and I am right, but nobody cares. Nobody listens to me. So what difference does it make?" Marshall was frustrated with the human condition.

"I see what you mean," Tom was listening. "What is the purpose of anything?"

"They don't teach us any of that in school," Marshall complained.

"Let life be your school. Learn from life," Tom advised.

"You don't know my life—my dad is in prison and my mom is crazy."

"Oh, your mom seems okay to me, just a bit unrealistic."

"It's more than that. You see, she has the temperament of an artist. She can't cope with our intensity and harshness. We are too rough and rowdy for her; we are out for the kill. She is becoming afraid of us as we grow into our power and manhood. It seems she would have been happier with little girls she could take into her sewing room and make cute dresses with bows and frills."

At War with Life

Tom reported back to Kriya, "I didn't know what to say to him. I don't think I was helpful."

"At least you began to dialogue with him. That is an opening. Let's have faith that all of us can live in peace in this house."

"Well, Kriya, have you overcome your fear of angry men? Find peace in your own heart first before you expect peace from others. Did you forgive your father for his outbursts of rage that made you cringe and hide?"

"After he died, I went to a psychic," she confided. "I can forgive him now because I have compassion and understanding. The medium explained that he was tormented by malicious spirits, especially late at night. He couldn't sleep as he festered in a quagmire of grievances over the imagined crimes of everyone he knew. He looked at life through a darkened lens and saw all people as his enemy."

"Do you see similar traits in Marshall and Malachi that you saw in your dad?" he asked.

"I see common ground: they are angry at life. My dad felt life treated him unfairly. He was not recognized by the world for his true greatness. 'I deserve better than this!' he would scream and pound his fist on the table. He felt his anger was justified and life was to blame for thwarting his ambitions."

"Go talk to Marshall," Tom suggested. "See if you can reach him. You are a woman, less threatening to his dominating male ego."

Wheel of Fortune

The next afternoon, after the teens returned home from school, Kriya knocked on Marshall's door. He was more than a bit surprised to see Kriya standing there. His wall of defense shot up. "What are you doing here?"

"We live down the hall from each other, and we don't know each other yet," she replied. Her apparent sincerity struck a resonant chord and he invited her in to his domain. On the floor, she noticed a spread of Tarot cards laid out in the formation of a cross, with the Wheel of Fortune card in reverse position. She thought, *I wonder what Fate has in store for us now. How much control do we really have? Or has the deck been dealt by the Hand of God and is being revealed to us each moment?*

"Can you read the cards?" she inquired, trying to connect with him.

"Sometimes," he replied cautiously. "It depends on how I feel that day."

"What is true on Monday may not be true on Tuesday?"

"Kind of like that. An orderly universe is but a dream in the minds of mad scientists. I favor the *chaos theory*. It applies to both absolute and relative universes, including our own," Marshall shared his perspective.

Chaos is not the Way of the Tao, she was thinking. Obviously, they did not agree. "Why live in chaos when you can live in order?" Kriya was curious.

"I like being unpredictable. It throws people off balance. I can do what I want when I want to. No rules except my own."

"I don't like being told how to live my life," Kriya sympathized.

"I get high on disrupting the system. It wasn't made for people like me. All those ridiculous rules that imprison your spirit and hold you back from the freedom of being yourself."

"So you are angry at the world?" Kriya put on her detective hat.

"The world is wrong and I am right," he asserted. "Maybe it wasn't designed by God, even though that's what everyone claims. Maybe we live in a random Universe. It just created itself out of nothing."

"If God created the Universe, would that justify its existence? If it was created by chance, does it have an equal right to exist?" Kriya questioned the nature of things.

"The Universe doesn't care. God doesn't care. It's all hype."

"I see your point of view," she acknowledged.

"My mom didn't care. Not when I was little and needed her to love me. Off she went in the summer months travelling from fair to fair, selling beadwork and dresses she made at home. We kids were a bother to her. We stood in the way of her dream-life because we were alive and real. She resented our interference in her plans."

"I think she was trying to earn a living to take care of you. She was a single mom doing her best to survive. Can you forgive her for neglecting you?"

"She was selfish!" he bristled. "My brother and I weren't important to her. We didn't count."

"When you look at her, what do you see?" asked Kriya.

"A frightened woman who hides behind a smile," he replied. "She is a good actress, very believable."

"She conjured up the world she lives in. She created a reality that suits her, a different reality than yours or mine," said Kriya.

"My reality is more important than yours or hers because it belongs to me. Your reality belongs to you. Her reality belongs to her. I warn you: don't take the rules of your reality and impose them on my world. I will listen but I will not obey!" he was adamant.

Kriya's Prayer

Kriya was thinking: *Maybe each of us is like Sunny, imagining our dream-world into existence. If every person creates their own unique reality, how are we all going to agree?* She shared her concerns with Tom: "Humanity cannot agree on which reality is real. No wonder we don't get along."

"We don't need to agree to get along. We can respect each person's point of view as being true for them. A little humility goes a long way in bringing peace to our planet," he said.

"It seems we live in bubbles hemmed in by our illusions," she said. "How do we escape from our dream-world and see clearly what actually is?"

"We need to let go of our beliefs and opinions and stop living in our minds. If people could access the wisdom of the heart, we could heal the conflicts created by the mind," Tom suggested. "Let's show compassion for Marshall and Malachi. Is there more we can do to turn them toward the Light? They are still young and capable of living honorable lives," Tom was sincere.

"Prayer is the answer. Let God intervene and work miracles of grace." Kriya believed in the power of prayer and the Love of God for everyone.

She reached under the bed and pulled out an old shoebox. Removing the lid, she gazed with satisfaction at her stash of healing stones and crystals. Closing her eyes, she slowly swept her hand over the stones until she could sense which ones called out to her, and she set these special stones aside.

Later that day, she placed them in the beaded pouch she wore around her neck and set out with a purpose in her heart. She headed for Silver Creek Park on the far side of town and followed the trail leading to her sacred healing place in the woods.

As the afternoon sun hung low in the sky, as the shadows grew long and darkened the landscape, Kriya lit a fire in the stone pit she used for ceremonies. As the sparks flew, her mind relaxed. Fire-gazing purified her spirit; she felt cleansed and renewed. In each hand she held a stone that infused her with fortitude to face what lay ahead.

Kriya prayed for the salvation of Marshall and Malachi.

Blessed Father of Creation,
Blessed Mother of Love,
I pray for healing for the hearts and souls of Marshall
*   and Malachi.*
I pray that God intervene to open their spiritual eyes so
*   they may see the Light.*
Amen.

Lady Justice

Malachi sat cross-legged on the floor, fixated on a wall hanging of Lady Justice. Her eyes shone gold with wisdom. In her right hand, she held the mighty Sword of Truth. In her left she held the scales that uphold the balance of Light and Dark. With a pleading heart, he probed her illumined eyes, searching for justice in a world gone mad. *Abracadabra,* he conjured up her presence to speak to him. *What is the key to my future?* he questioned the Lady of Fairness and Balance.

Young man, she replied, *you stand at a crossroads. Do you continue on the path of anger, or do you choose to walk in the Light? Which way do you go?*

Malachi walked over to the mirror and reflected on his self-image. Who was he, really? He was thinking, *Anger makes me feel alive. It is a kind of power to scare people and make them cringe. The Light is overwhelming. It is too bright for my eyes.*

His heart was hurting from the pain of rejection. Life had abandoned him. Society scorned him. Of course his anger was justified. Of course. He identified with his anger; it gave him his sense of self. He thought. *"Where was the Light when I needed it? How can I trust the Light?*

Lady Justice held up the Sword of Truth and a blue flame shot into the room. Malachi was awestruck. He felt the Light of Truth strike a chord in his heart. A shift in perception. He realized, *The power of the Light is greater than the power of anger. Am I ready to face the Light?*

His moment of choice had arrived.

Destiny is Calling

*S*lam! went the front door and in swept the Wind, on the prowl, charging ahead, looking to stir up trouble. *Whissh Ho! Whoa Ha!* The Wind mocked all pretense of normality. The status quo was the favorite target of the rebellious Wind.

Under the stairwell was a network of dust-covered webbing wherein dwelt the spirit critters of the shadow world hiding from the light of day. A nest of astral spiders flew apart when the Wind gusted in their midst.

A young one of the spirit critters lost his grip and fell down to the floor. Separated from his own kind, he felt so alone. "Help me!" he cried out in fear. Ever on the alert, Princess sensed his distress and came to the rescue.

"It's no accident that we meet today. Destiny is calling you. A higher path awaits you if you make the choice to be free," she declared.

"Oh, no. We are not allowed to choose. We must follow orders."

"I am a cat and I can choose." Princess was proud of her feline identity.

"We cannot. It is set up that way," he objected.

"What is your name, little one?"

"I do not have a name. We are not permitted to be individuals. We cannot think for ourselves."

"I shall give you a name," she offered.

"A name? Just for me!" The little one was delighted.

"I shall call you 'Seeker,' because you are searching to find your way. The path to Liberation is the universal call. God is calling all beings everywhere to return home to Love."

"I don't know anything about love. Love does not exist in our reality," he frowned.

"Love is God's Heart. Feel it now." Princess opened her heart and sent a beam of God's love to the seemingly helpless creature crying out for salvation. "Love is here. Love will take you home."

The little seeker began to cry, "I never felt that before," he said in astonishment. "I didn't know I had a heart."

"God's love can heal you. Love is the miracle alive in our hearts."

Time to Fly

Up the stairs the Wind swished and swirled into the bathroom by the landing. Under the bathtub it gushed through the hole and up to the rafters to where Tiger hid.

"What brings you hither, O Spirit of the Wind?" he inquired.

"I shall blow away the cobwebs of your mind that keep you in bondage to the past. I am the Force of Change."

The Wind called to Tiger:

> *Come fly with me.*
> *Release old concepts of reality.*
> *Come play with me.*
> *Be free like I am free.*

With these words, the Wind whisked itself away.

Tiger considered the message of the fearless Wind. Memories from his early days in NoMan's Land flashed into his mind. He remembered cringing in fear in the shadows of the stockade, not knowing what lay ahead. He remembered that decisive moment when he pulled open the gate and saw the light shining through, beckoning him to escape into the Land of Light and Freedom. (See Book One.)

It is the moment of choice. I can no longer delay my decision. Shall I return to the confines of the attic room? Or dare I break free and face the unknown? I am being called to fulfill my destiny. What grand adventures await me? He realized, *My retreat has allowed me time to ponder on the purpose of my life: I shall teach peace and live it from the heart.*

He thought, *The Wind is free to come and free to go. I will fly like the Wind.*

God Bless America

Tiger was lean from days of fasting. He knew it was time to leave his hideaway and get on with his life. Slowly he edged his way along the sturdy beam and down the post he climbed, crawling through the gap in the insulation. He crept through the darkness until he spotted rays of light, which drew him onward until he found the hole under the bathtub and squirmed his way through, emerging from his retreat with a renewed lease on life.

It was late at night when Tiger approached the TV nook. *Zing! Bang! Boom!* He heard a sputter of gunshots coming from the television set. Slinking behind the bookcase, he watched Marshall and Malachi engrossed in the drama projected on the screen.

A news commentator interrupted the show with a live bulletin. With an undertone of fear, he announced: "A bomb detonated by agents of evil has blown apart the American Embassy in Mizar. The Emissaries of Darkness have claimed responsibility. Future attacks are imminent unless humanity forfeits its free will and turns away from God." A fiery explosion lit up the screen, with billows of black smoke and screaming embassy workers fleeing in terror. The gremlets cheered and clapped their hands, applauding their sinister astral allies who instigated this assault on America's might and power. *Strike back! Attack!* they shouted in unison as they aimed their megaphones at adolescent ears.

Marshall was awestruck by the immense tragedy he saw unfolding before his eyes. "I shall enlist in the army and annihilate our enemies. God bless America!" he shouted, stoked up with anger that justified revenge.

Malachi was not convinced. "War is against my conscience. My heart says *No!*"

"Wow. Have you changed!" Marshall was flabbergasted.

"I see life differently now. I was fooling myself before. I was afraid to see."

From his hiding place behind the bookcase, Tiger observed the scene. He decided, *I must go out into the world and change the mind-set that leads to war. I have a mission to accomplish. Cats can save the world!*

Tiger Meets Daniel

Seeking relief from the angst in the TV nook, Tiger slipped out from behind the bookcase, turned the corner, and walked into the kitchen. Ravenously hungry, he jumped on the counter and devoured tidbits of leftovers from that night's dinner. At last he was ready for the next step in his life adventure, to take a leap into the unknown as he had done as a kitten when he escaped the stockade.

Tiger was heading for the back door, his logical escape route. He entered the utility room and pushed up against the back door with all his might, trying to budge it open. To no avail. *I must wait until morning*, he realized, *when Sunny washes the laundry and unlocks the door.*

Tiger wandered into the art museum, found a comfortable chair, curled up and took a nap. Soon he was sleeping soundly under the watchful eyes of the ladies and gentlemen residing in Sunny's portraits. The sensation of a cold hand stroking his fur awakened him from his dreamtime. Tiger looked up and saw an ethereal-looking man of serious demeanor.

"I am Daniel, Sunny's uncle and friend," he introduced himself, speaking in the subdued tones of the world beyond.

"I am Tykee the Tiger, Tom and Kriya's cat," Tiger replied. "Are you a ghost or a real person?"

"Ghosts are real people. We have thoughts and personalities, just like living people," he responded.

"How do you know which thoughts are your thoughts?" Tiger dared to ask this provocative question.

"Ah so! You have met the terrorist twins, Alderon and Algenon, I presume."

"Yes. They ignite sparks of anger that inflame the minds of young rebels," Tiger observed. "They project menacing thoughts into their minds, inciting them to quarrel and fight."

"The gremlets sustain themselves with an energy source called *leuch*," Daniel explained. "They obtain their food supply from human beings by evoking low vibration emotions."

"Their game is war and violence. I'd rather play tag." Tiger was appalled.

"It is their nature. They are programmed to disrupt and dismay."

"Last night I watched Marshall and Malachi succumbing to the spell of the mainstream media," Tiger reported. "As the TV blared news of an attack by our enemies, the boys' attention was captured by the drama and magnitude of the event. Watching the flames of our embassy burning, they became mesmerized, glued to their seats."

"Frames of subliminals were interspersed with the footage of the fires," Daniel explained. "Images of fire reach deep into the primordial unconscious."

Tiger continued his report: "The astute gremlets telepathically picked up the words broadcast from the subliminals and repeated them in the boys' ears. Marshall was persuaded; he is planning to enlist in the army."

Daniel responded, "Marshall is an unknowing victim of the system he rebels against. He is being used as a pawn of the war machine. The Controllers are targeting the vulnerable minds of America for their will to be done."

"How do you know so much? Are you a psychiatrist?"

"No. But I studied psychology when I worked for the government. I was solicited to become part of a secret program sponsored by the Department of Defense. We set up an experimental laboratory to test subjects' responses to frequency stimulation. The goal was to engineer societal programming to steal people's freedom by surreptitiously undermining their power of choice. The media encourages people to make choices from fear-based emotions rather than from love, wisdom, and compassion."

"I'm glad I am a cat. The human drama is bizarre, with all the games and subterfuge." Tiger valued his feline identity. "Cats are psychic and intuitive. We are neither run by our emotions, nor fooled by our thoughts."

"If you want to explore the kinds of thinking that lead to war, if you want to consider the ways of living that lead to peace, you must meet my longtime friend Salmun. He writes documentaries that tell the truth as he sees it about what is really going on. Before I was murdered, I gave him my research notes on the state of mind control in America. I am sure the technology of mass deception has advanced by leaps and bounds since my death."

"How do I find him?"

"He lives in a backwoods cabin in the forestlands north of Meridian. I shall send Tula, my guide bird, to fly just ahead of you to lead the way to Salmun's retreat. Tula is an astral bird who can see our world."

"Thank you so much! " Tiger was grateful "This is my next step."

Old Snarly

Tiger spent the night in the utility room awaiting Sunny's arrival in the morn to unlatch the back door. As the hours passed, he contemplated his future. *I must find Salmun,* he decided, *and learn from him the ways of peace that can bring healing to the world.*

The golden glow of sunlight streamed through the lace curtains and highlighted the latticework of cobwebs suspended from the ceiling. Sunny arrived bright and early, singing as she worked. Carrying the laundry basket with both hands, she went into the yard to hang the damp clothes on the line, leaving the door slightly ajar. The opportune moment had arrived! Tiger dashed outside into the unknown. Quick as a wink, he ran down the hillside into a grove of aspens, their white trunks gleaming in the light of a new day. He climbed to the topmost branch of the tallest tree and surveyed the scene from a birds-eye vantage point.

Which way to go?
He did not know.

From his lookout perch above the rooftops, his watchful eyes scanned the skies, hoping to spot the guide bird that would lead him to the next stage of his life. *Will he be a shining black raven, or perhaps a mighty hawk?*

Tiger took a deep breath and inhaled the fragrant essence of the sun-lit morn. The birds sang songs of freedom that inspired trust in the flow of Life. The Wind danced in circles around the aspen grove, celebrating his escape from the dark domain.

Slinking along a rickety rail fence marking the border of Sunny's property, the top cat of the territory was on the prowl. Old Snarly had a scruffy orange coat and an ornery disposition. His whiskers were gnarled and twisted, the corner of his left ear ripped off in a fray. He was ready to pick a fight to prove himself as the unrivaled king of the heap. Old Snarly sang his song:

> *I'm Old Snarly, the sour puss.*
> *I'm nasty and I'm mean.*
> *Stay out of my territory.*
> *I'm the boss of this scene.*

The orange bully jumped off the fence and hid in a thicket, poised to attack the intruder. As Tiger climbed down from his lookout and set his paws on Mother Earth, Old Snarly charged at him with feline fury. *Nee'eh! Nee'eh!* he snarled. *Get out and stay out! This is my domain!* He chased him over the fence, across the road and far, far away.

Tiger kept running and running until Sunny's house was but a memory.

To be continued in Book Three of
Cats Can Save the World

Afterword

Living in Integrity

We live in pivotal times. The choices we make now will steer the course of humanity for years to come. The potential to create a sane, just and loving world for everyone lies in the hearts and minds of each individual.

To create a world of peace and compassion, we need to live in integrity and keep our minds open. That entails the courage to venture into the unknown and give up what we think we know. We need to see without the filter of our conditioned beliefs and attitudes.

Living in integrity requires our willingness to overcome our fear of seeing the truth. Let us let go of beliefs that foster a culture of denial. When we turn away and avoid, we are allowing the hidden agenda to flourish in plain sight. What is our level of commitment to seeing the world as it actually is? Are we willing to look at what we do not like, and to expand our horizons of what we believe can be possible? Do we tune out information that doesn't line up with our cherished beliefs about what is real and what can be? The culture of denial is preventing humanity from bringing in more Light.

Let us hold dear our divine right of free will, and not allow it to be undermined by covert influences seeking to limit and control us. It is imperative we make choices as sovereign individuals who have examined the contents of our minds. Self-monitoring and vigilance are keys to ensuring we withstand any attempts to lead us astray.

Many are being called to serve as midwives of change, assisting the birth of a new society based on love and unity. For peace to prevail on Earth, let us assume responsibility for our state of mind and consciousness. The clear seeing of an awakened heart can offer protection from the sway of dark power. Cultivating a compassionate heart will help humanity rise above the fear-based agenda. We must not underestimate the power of the heart to change everything.

My Perspective

My personal encounters with the Dark side through many years have motivated me to put into writing what I have learned and what I am learning now. I don't want people to suffer the way I did because of my ignorance of the *modus operandi* of negative entities. Knowledge *is* power. The more we know about how they operate, the less they will be able to manipulate and control us. Years ago, I thought I was free, but looking back, I realize that I wasn't. Because I didn't know then what I know now.

I learned that we are multi-dimensional beings, and we interact with the spirit world more than we realize. We draw to us beings that resonate with our thoughts and emotions, and with the frequencies we are emitting. Negative entities are attracted by our pain and disenchantment with life. By preying upon our weaknesses, they call to our attention those wounded places within us, which can motivate us to heal and develop strength of character.

We also attract beings of Light who offer guidance, healing, and protection, and who inspire us with expanded possibilities.

Not everyone is influenced by negative entities, but some of us are, some of the time. It a subject worth exploring as an investigation into our psyche to see if we are operating as free and sovereign beings. How we make our choices is our responsibility. At this pivotal time of collective decision-making, let us make choices that come from the heart. The co-creative power of humanity can turn the tide for truth.

The Dark and the Light enact the roles of adversaries in the Earth School play of life. The Dark challenges us to keep our hearts open. The Dark tests our will and commitment to truth. When the lessons of the Dark are embraced and learned from, we are not victims but masters of the game of duality.

Acknowledgements

I wish to honor all brave souls who dare to take a stand for Freedom and Justice at this critical time when the truth is being suppressed and our civil liberties are being curtailed. It takes courage to stand up against the rising tide of censorship and express the truth as you believe in your heart.

In my community of Ashland, Oregon, I wish to acknowledge Jason and Vanessa Houk (Jobs with Justice), whose compassionate hearts serve the poor and homeless residents of our town; Avram Sacks (Jewish Voices for Peace), who advocates for the human rights of the Palestinian people; and Gangaji, whose transmission of love is the highest calling. I recommend her booklet, *Our Responsibility for Peace*.

In addition, I wish to thank David Wick, co-founder of the Ashland Culture of Peace Commission, and the dedicated volunteers, who are striving for greater harmony and inclusivity in our community. I am grateful to the citizens of Jackson County, Oregon, for passing an ordinance banning GMO food, setting a precedent for our nation. I wish to honor the mothers and the fathers, the teachers, the healers, the journalists and the whistleblowers—all beings committed to bringing Light to our planet and evoking compassion in our hearts.

I wish to honor my beloved cat Tykee the Tiger, an enlightened soul, who freely and effortlessly expressed the joy of being. I give thanks to Princess, who demonstrated a cat's love of adventure, and to quiet Mirabel, an example of patience and perseverance. My cats have been my teachers of unconditional love and living in the moment.

The cover artwork was inspired by a photo by Shannon Story and created by my artist-friend, Robert Bissett, my neighbor when I lived in Idaho. God has sent me an angel in the form of Nancy Kionke, a pleasure to work with, who has diligently applied herself to copyediting and formatting the interior. I am grateful to Avram Sacks for his loving support, and to Jasmin Lace for the author photo. I want to acknowledge my other copyeditor, Leslie Caplan, also of Ashland, for her fine-tuned skill in ferreting out errors and omissions.

I wish to thank all of you, the readers, for making your unique contribution to the world. The future is in your hands. May you choose wisely.

Made in the USA
Columbia, SC
07 July 2018